W9-DDA-821

GIDEON

GIDEON

A Novel
by Chester Aaron

J. B. LIPPINCOTT   New York

The "young man" incident on page 49, chapter 5, is an altered version of an incident in *For Those I Loved,* by Martin Gray (with Max Gallo). Gideon's meeting with the gang, also in chapter 5, owes much to a similar meeting in *For Those I Loved.* I am indebted to Dan Kurzman's *The Bravest Battle* for the facts about Captain Henry Iwanski in chapter 9.

I am grateful to Bernard Goldstein for permission to reprint material from *The Stars Bear Witness* on pp. 116–17 and 118; to Jean François Steiner for permission to reprint material from *Treblinka* on pp. 151–56.

Library of Congress Cataloging in Publication Data

Aaron, Chester.
Gideon.

SUMMARY: After losing family and friends, Gideon
must bury religion and identity in order to survive
the Warsaw ghetto and Treblinka concentration camp
during World War II.
    [1. Holocaust, Jewish (1939–1945)—Fiction.
2. Jews—Poland—Fiction.   3. World War, 1939–1945—
Poland—Fiction]   I. Title.
PZ7.A12Gi 1982   [Fic]   81–48066
                                  AACR2
ISBN 0-397-31992-4   ISBN 0-397-31993-2 (lib. bdg.)

1 2 3 4 5 6 7 8 9 10
First Edition

For Tsvicka and Chatskel
Alevasholem

Preface

I was not in the Warsaw ghetto. I was not a prisoner in Treblinka. I was with the American troops that opened the gates at Dachau.

In writing this novel I have relied on conversations I had in May and June of 1945 with survivors of Dachau, and on several conversations I since have had in the United States and Israel with men and women who had been children or adolescents in German concentration camps.

Journals, diaries, reflections, and histories that I have read since 1945, many written by survivors, have supplemented those conversations.

Of all that I have read, I am grateful to and especially recommend:

The Warsaw Ghetto, by Reuben Ainsztein (Holocaust Library, N.Y.)

The Holocaust Kingdom, by Alexander Donat (Holocaust Library, N.Y.)

The Death Camp Treblinka, edited by Alexander Donat (Holocaust Library, N.Y.)

From Bergen-Belsen to Jerusalem, by Emil Fackenheim (Institute of Contemporary Jewry, Hebrew University of Jerusalem)

Young Moshe's Diary, by Moshe Flinker (Yad Vashem, Jerusalem)

The Stars Bear Witness, by Bernard Goldstein (Viking Press)

For Those I Loved, by Martin Gray with Max Gallo (Little Brown and Company)

The Bravest Battle, by Dan Kurzman (G.P. Putnam)

On Both Sides of the Wall, by Vladka Meed (Holocaust Library, N.Y.)

The Yellow Star, by Gerhard Schoenberner (Bantam Books)

Treblinka, by Jean Francois Steiner (Simon and Schuster)

The Death Brigade, by Leon W. Wells (Holocaust Library, N.Y.)

The Holocaust (Yad Vashem, Jerusalem)

Many of the characters in this novel did exist. Several of the characters are created from shadows. Gideon's life is a combination of fact and fiction, of events that did or could have happened to millions of children in Europe.

Unfortunately, the history, as recorded, is a matter of public record.

GIDEON

Do ye hear the children weeping, O my
brothers . . .
    . . . the young, young children, O my brothers,
    They are weeping bitterly!
They are weeping in the playtime of the others. . . .
                        —Elizabeth Barrett Browning,
                        "The Cry of the Children"

1

Now and then the will to survive weakened, but it never died. Along with that will to survive there was, during those years, much good luck.

My hair, for example. It has always been straight, always the color of hay. When I was a child before the war, my mother and grandmother competed with each other to best describe the blue of my eyes. Sky blue, ocean blue, the blue of a violet, of an iris.

I never looked like a Jew. In those days that could only be fortunate.

There you are. Now you know.

Why didn't I ever tell you?

That, I think, is one of the reasons I have written

this for you. But I am not being honest. I have not written this just for you. I have written it for myself as well.

Where shall I begin? Before or after I entered the ghetto? After. For good reason. My life before I was twelve lost significance. It ended so quickly, so completely that, like many children in Warsaw, I considered myself as having been born inside the ghetto walls.

Now, this moment, as I begin writing, the first scene that rises before me occurred in July, 1942. Before the uprising. I am fourteen, and I have already lived in the ghetto since November, 1940.

There is a cluster of Jews at the gate near Tlomackie. German soldiers force the Jews to take off their clothes and dance. Other Jews nearby are commanded to sing and applaud. I stand among them. Outside the gate, a group of Poles have gathered to observe the entertainment.

For eight months I have been escaping the ghetto and going to Aryan Warsaw (called this because all of Warsaw outside the ghetto had been "cleansed" of Jews). I have been meeting with One-Eye and his gang since April. We—the gang and I—have an alliance that profits both them and us, the Jews in the ghetto. I am scheduled to meet with One-Eye in an hour.

A soldier pushes into the crowd and grabs a man whose hair had obviously been shorn recently, in the last hour or so. A few twisted curls still cling to his collar. The skin where there had been a beard for fifty or sixty years is much lighter than the rest of his face. Recent razor cuts on his chin and neck are still oozing blood. His panicked attempt to save himself has only succeeded in drawing attention to himself, in provoking the anger of the Germans.

They hurl the old man at the dancers, knocking several down. The old man's body slides across the cobblestones. The soldiers jerk him upright, and a young German officer with red hair and freckles orders him to dance. The old man balances on one foot. Beg, the officer demands, beg your master. The old Jew lifts his nose into the air, and he whines and wriggles his hands. When the Poles laugh and applaud, I force myself to laugh too. I have long ago learned how essential it is to accept humiliation in order to survive.

Soldiers appear from the side streets and from behind us. And four trucks.

I have been confronting such crises daily, almost

hourly, ever since I started leaving the ghetto. My luck, my cunning, my sharply honed reflexes have always saved me. This time I have delayed seconds too long. With the other Jews I am packed into the trucks. A few Poles have been swept up as well. They protest. They are not Jews. They hate Jews. They have always hated Jews. The Germans ignore their pleas.

There is little correspondence between age and survival instincts in the ghetto. I and those other children who have survived possess a greater store of knowledge and devices for survival than most adults do.

Reaching into my pocket, I remove my armband, which defines me as a Jew. During the next several minutes, I rip the cloth apart with my nails and force the fragments into my mouth. By the time the trucks stop, I have eaten the entire armband. Now my counterfeit papers and the silver medal of the Virgin Mary around my neck should satisfy the Germans that I am a Catholic.

When we reach Szczesliwice Station, the soldiers begin yelling, pounding heads and shoulders with rifle butts, firing into the air, driving us out of the trucks and onto the platform of the *Umschlagplatz*— the collecting station—and into the cattle cars. Other

Jews, brought earlier, are already in the cars. Women and men faint, but our bodies are packed so closely together, the unconscious victims are unable to fall to the floor.

I feel fresh air on my legs. The grating! Such openings were built into the walls of these cars, near the floors, so the confined cattle could receive enough air to survive their journey to the slaughterhouses.

A woman next to me—one of the Poles who had screamed her hatred of Jews—has turned blue, almost purple. She has stopped breathing but remains upright.

I fight to a stooped position, use my knife and fingers. After ten or fifteen minutes I have the grating out of its frame. It takes several minutes to writhe and slide to the floor, to double myself up, to get my head through the opening. I push with my feet against the legs of the Jews around me and squeeze my body, inch by inch, through the hole. When I fall, I let my body roll.

The train slows. There are several shots. A burst of shots. Many bursts. For a moment I regret my escape. Because I have escaped, the Germans are shooting other Jews. *Survive, Gideon . . . at any cost . . .*

Will they be saved if I surrender? No.

7

Often at such moments, when I have doubts, when I begin to falter, my father's voice seeks me out, as if it is always waiting to be needed. *The important thing, Gideon, is to survive. In any way, at any cost, survive. By surviving you can not only fight back, you can carry the story of what is happening in this ghetto. The world must know. You and others must tell. You are of no use to our people dead.*

I jump up from the cinders. Ahead and behind me the guns are still firing. I run and hide, regain my strength, and run and hide again.

I find a farm, and the peasants help me. While I eat their bread and soup, they talk about how bad things have become. Ah, but everything will improve once the Jews have been wiped out. Then the Germans will leave Poland. When I tell them what has just happened, that I have almost been taken with Jews to be killed, that several Poles had also been killed, they shake their fingers at me. I am, they warn me, very young, very innocent. I should have known that all I had to do was to show my medal to the soldiers. They would not have bothered me. They're only after Jews, thank God. And what was I doing in the ghetto anyway? Ah, my parents and my priest have sadly neglected my education. With a final warning to stay away from the Jews, the peasants give me directions back to Warsaw. They also give me more bread. And a few zlotys in case I want to buy some cheese.

2

In Warsaw, I find my way back to Tlomackie, like a fragment of metal drawn to a magnet. Two guards are standing under the lights, concentrating on a magazine, groaning and nudging each other and laughing. I move past them like a ghost.

It is dark. The streets are empty except for two Jewish policemen leaning against a wall. I know the streets and their shadows far too well to let the policemen see me.

My first stop is Gliniana, near the Jewish cemetery, in a cellar beneath an enormous warehouse. I descend the stairs, knock once, wait, knock once, wait, knock twice. The door opens. Yankele stands in the doorway, his body almost filling the space. He tries to look serious but cannot carry it off. He laughs, grabs me, lifts me as if I were a puppy, and carries me inside. There, at the table, hovering over a map of Warsaw, sits One-Eye. He too plays at being serious, being angry. "So," he says, "I dodge the Germans for nothing."

Yankele closes and locks the door. "Ah," he says, taking a bottle of vodka from a crate, "practice makes perfect."

Before our third glass, when I tell them I should go to my parents to reassure them, Yankele informs me that he has sent a message to my father, letting him know that one of the sharp-eyed porters in our organization had seen me being taken to the *Umschlagplatz,*

After several detours, I reach our apartment building on Nowolipki. The door to our fifth floor apartment is closed. I knock. There is no sound behind the door. I knock again. Still no sound. Having lived through this experience many times—that knock on the door in the middle of the night—I know what terrors have been aroused inside the room. If anyone is still there. Has my father gone out to try to find me? Has the Gestapo taken everyone—my mother, my father, my cousins, my aunts and uncles? Has my mother, in one more effort to outwit the network of spies and police, Jewish and German, rushed everyone to a different apartment?

I knock again, trying to soften the impact of my knuckles. "It's me, Gideon."

The door is flung open. "He's safe!" my father cries. He has a German Luger in his hand. He pushes the weapon inside his belt and embraces me.

Everyone is laughing or weeping. They hug me, demand a touch, a pinch, to verify my existence. My mother kisses my cheeks, my mouth, the top of my head, making up in one moment for weeks of declining attention. In this moment, the fatigue and despair that have reduced my mother to an almost unrecognizable shadow of her old self are replaced by an energy that seems to rekindle the former fire in her eyes.

Though for some time now I have not been considered the respectable model for my young cousins (or for other children in the ghetto), my cousins and uncles and aunts settle around the table, some on chairs, some on the floor, and insist I tell my story.

You should know that at this point—late July, 1942—out of the approximately eighty close relatives we had in Poland before the German invasion, less than thirty remain alive. Of those thirty, nine are in this room. They, and my mother and father, are waiting.

After Yankele informed my father that I'd been taken to the *Umschlagplatz,* there was general mourning. It is common knowledge now that departure from the *Umschlagplatz* means a factory or a death camp. Either means doom. At a factory I'd work until I died of starvation or exhaustion; at a camp I'd be gassed and cremated.

But here I am. Safe. Escaped. How, Gideon?

My father stares at me as I tell what happened. He seems surprised at the appearance of such strong survival instincts. I have completed the conversion from a meek little *yeshiva bukher* to a tough guerrilla fighter. My mother shifts uncomfortably in her chair when he actually says this, but her discomfort does not quite conceal her pride. Even had she disagreed strongly, she would not have spoken out. Once, long ago, she would have, but not now. These days she rarely speaks to anyone about anything.

My father's surprise is understandable. He has always considered me, like a himself, a scholar. Now, like he, the scholar has become a man of action. I was always a good student, learning languages easily, always serious about going to *cheder,* studying Hebrew and the Torah. But I never considered myself a dedicated scholar, a *yeshiva bukher.*

After I tell my story, there is silence, awe, admiration. The Germans have been cheated out of one of us. Then several relatives urge my father to tell what had happened to him. He hesitates. Another time would be better. Everyone is exhausted. This is Gideon's night. But my mother's quiet voice suggests that tonight is as good as any other night, and he relents.

A few hours before my safe return, my father and two comrades managed to travel to the Warsaw suburbs. Their routes were secured by bribed Polish officials and policemen who several times before had guided them out of the ghetto to meet in Aryan Warsaw with members of the Polish underground. There they would procure weapons or discuss tactics to be used against the occupying German army. This evening, at a restaurant, an arrest was attempted and my father killed a German officer—one of the very worst butchers of Jews. "A bonus," my father says, holding up the Luger. It had been the butcher's.

In prompt retaliation, the Germans executed fifty Jews, hauling them out of rooms and shooting them in the street. The fifty included eleven children.

Each such operation from now on, my father predicts, will be costlier. Reciprocity by the Germans will grow more severe. But—and he holds the Luger above his head—we are fighting back. The Jews are fighting back.

My mother's grim, gray face brightens. For one moment I see the pride and beauty I'd known all those years I was growing up.

In the small apartment in which fourteen of us sleep—twelve relatives and two friends—my father preens himself like an animal after a successful battle. My mother's eyes betray her anxiety. She has always scorned passivity, but my father's flamboyant disdain for danger frightens her now. Twenty months in the ghetto have taken a heavy toll not just of her face and body but of her mind as well. For the first time I smell despair, as if her body gives it off as a scent.

After the stories of my escape and my father's killing of the German butcher circulate through the ghetto, a group gathers in our apartment to consider the consequences. Has the one retaliation satisfied the Germans?

Fifty Jews for one German, my Aunt Pola mutters. Such a terrible price to pay.

Isaac Lewenthal, who, until the invasion, had been

15

a professor of mathematics at Krakow University, says that at this rate my father and his vengeance-crazed comrades will quickly succeed in doing the Germans' work for them. By the time one thousand such Germans have been murdered, the Jewish population will be wiped out.

My father's question is subdued. "What are you saying? Are you saying we should not fight back?"

Isaac Lewenthal shrugs. "I leave philosophy to philosophers. I'm a mathematician. I deal with number theories."

"The Germans," my father says, calm, his patience forced, "no longer let you deal only with number theories. Numbers? All right. One hundred. A nice round number. Give me one hundred rifles and one hundred fighters."

"You would lose. Eventually you would lose. Speak to the corpses in the streets."

"Every day, every night, those corpses speak to me. Tell me, Isaac: doing nothing, not fighting back, do we win?"

"We will all be dead. Will that satisfy you?"

"And if we accept whatever they do and we don't fight back, some of us will live? Who? How many? Do you want to be one of those who survive after everyone else in this room has been killed?"

"The Polish underground . . ."

My father throws up his hands, exasperated. He closes his right fist and extends his little finger. "This much. The Polish underground helps us this much. You want to wait until someone rescues us? Who will rescue us, whatever is left of us? Roosevelt? Stalin? Stalin is a Russian; you think he loves Jews? Roosevelt is a politician; he needs votes, that great humanitarian. Do you vote in America, Isaac?"

"You will kill us all. Is that what you want?"

"No." My mother's voice sounds as if great effort has been required to make the word audible. "That is not what Jacob wants. It is not what I want. I want us all to live. But all of us will not live. Look around you. Count. How many of your family, of your friends, are still alive? What I want and what you want means nothing. Nothing. The Germans decide if we live or die. Most of us, maybe all of us, will die. Me, you, Jacob, Gideon, my mother, my little Sonia." I hear my father's breath catch in his throat, but my mother continues. "Isaac, my dear friend, we have little to leave Gideon, but if he remembers us as Jews who fought, who resisted extermination, well, there could be worse things than dying."

"Such heroics. Such theater."

"No. Not heroics, not theater. Facts."

My father cups her chin in his hand. "All her life she's known courage. It has taken me all my life to discover it."

I am not saddened by the thought of their death; I am disgusted by their acceptance of the inevitability of it. Since the day I arrived in the ghetto, death has been so large a presence in my life it is no longer important enough to dread. It is only another danger to avoid, an obstacle to overcome, a clerk or a policeman or a soldier to bribe. To witness my mother and father yield to it as if there were no way to evade it, to deny it, to outwit it, pains me more than the thought that, being dead, they will be gone from my life.

I discover a sleeping place on the floor near my father. We share the blanket. He shifts his Luger so it will not lie between us, and he drops his arm across my body. There are three shots outside. My father's body jerks with each shot as if his own body has been struck. Silence. Then someone in the room, in the darkness—my Uncle Mordecai, I think—begins to pray. It is the Kaddish, the prayer for the dead.

"You will survive," my father whispers. "You must."

Somewhere far off in the ghetto, a burst of gunfire. Two and then three voices chant the Kaddish.

I draw my father's arm close about me. We have all been so absorbed in what we've been doing these past months, we've permitted ourselves no time for conversation.

"Gideon."

"Yes, Father?"

"Shh, not so loud. This gang you are with. They are Poles?"

"Yes."

"And this porter, this Yankele, the smuggler . . ."

Ah, finally. After all this time.

"He is a Jew," my father whispers, "who cares nothing about Jews."

"He cares about me. He and the gang—those Poles—would have tried to rescue me even if it meant death for them. Just as I'd try to rescue them if they were captured."

"I wish I would see in you such strong loyalty to the Jews."

I want to leap up and run from the room. What

would he say, what would he do, if I were to reply no, I feel no such loyalty to Jews? What would he say, what would he do, if I were to tell him I'm sick of being a Jew, sick of being reminded that the word *Jew* is a synonym for the word *death*? Being a Jew means children stretched out in the streets; being a Jew means freezing in dark rooms, picking lice from your hair, rotting in gutters. What would he say, what would he do, if I were to scream out I DON'T WANT TO BE A JEW! I HATE BEING A JEW!?

"The man will contaminate you, Gideon. You too will soon be nothing but a thug, a smuggler. He has a history, long before the ghetto . . ."

I breathe deeply, as if I've fallen asleep. And then I hear a terrible thing. My father is weeping. What can I do but turn to face him, to take him in my arms as if he were the child and I the man? Are those muted sobs in the corner of the room coming from my mother?

A shot outside, close to our building. A scream. Two shots. Again, in the room, Kaddish.

3

I have to go back in time now, in history. Writers of novels would call it a flashback. Certain details are necessary here, details about the place, about the time, about my parents, your grandparents.

Unlike most mothers—before, in peacetime Warsaw, or now, in the ghetto—my mother was never uncertain or uneasy about Jews asserting themselves, Jews being physically aggressive. She scorned the old myth that Jews should never offend Gentiles, should not arouse their hostility. She was never submissive to relatives, friends, neighbors, strangers. In response to cautious questions she would say, with

21

a toss of her long brown hair, "I am a Jew." Emphasizing the word *Jew*. With her small, delicate body and her pale face, she seemed to have insisted on retaining positive Semitic identity in her nose, which had that distinct hook cartoonists mocked in every German newspaper.

"Where did you come from? Did you come from the moon?" That was part of a song she used to sing while feeding my little sister, Sonia, who was as blond, as blue-eyed, as any Aryan fraülein. Look at her, my grandmother used to urge anyone within calling distance. Sit little Sonia to the right of Hitler and Gideon to the left and tell me: who is more Aryan?

Like a few other Jews, my grandmother continued to live outside the ghetto, in Aryan Warsaw, in the apartment house she'd owned for thirty years. It was from her that Sonia and I inherited our blond hair and our blue eyes and straight noses. It was from her that my mother had inherited the independence that used to make my father wince. No, not independence. Pride. Ah, but in those days before the war, before the ghetto, Gentiles often saw that independence, that pride, as arrogance. Here in the ghetto, as my mother surrendered that independence, that pride, my father assumed it. Now he is one of the organizers of the Defense Committee. He is so aggressive, so militant, that other members of the committee often have to restrain him. A lion of Judah, my Aunt Pola calls him now. My Aunt Pola has always been famous for her sharp tongue. Before we entered the ghetto, she says, he was a timid house cat.

Before—before the ghetto, before the Germans invaded Poland—our neighborhood, a mix of Jew and Gentile, bordered an exclusively Gentile neighborhood. Most Jewish students attended the public schools, but my mother decided I ought to spend my fifth grade in one of the private Gentile schools. My father protested at first. Of the fifty students in my class, only three, including me, would be Jews. Almost as bad: there would be classes on Saturdays. For my mother and father, Saturday was a holy day, a part of the Sabbath.

My mother persisted. Times were changing, she argued. I should receive a more general education than other Jewish children were receiving. For a Jew to endure in the changing world, he must learn sophistication when very young.

My father's resistance was finally worn down. He agreed that yes, it could be to my benefit to meet

Gentiles I'd be working with when I was older. To be involved in publishing, as he was, I should cultivate my flair for languages, be at ease with various kinds of people, help build bridges between countries and cultures. But not at the expense of my own heritage.

That summer before I transferred to the Gentile school, I studied Hebrew and the Torah. And while I attended the school, time had to be found so I might continue to prepare for my bar mitzvah.

I was blond and blue-eyed like all the Gentile children in that school, but of course everyone knew I was a Jew. When the students and teachers made cruel jokes about Jews, the butt of the jokes was some anonymous Jew outside my skin, outside the room, in some distant country. I neither looked nor talked like a Jew. But when I heard these jokes and when the other boys teased me and beat me up, I knew the Jew in those jokes was me.

Welcome to the world, my mother said. But unlike my cousins, who learned passive acceptance as they learned their Hebrew, I, she said, should fight back. No, my father said, a few cannot fight many. I insisted I was not afraid to fight, but I was. I was strong, I said. I wasn't. I never was and never will be big and strong. A fact that led to my early reliance on other abilities.

My father was famous for his quiet, slightly pedantic manner. He rarely raised his voice, even when annoyed or angry. But when I came home one day with my clothes torn, bruises on my face, bragging that I'd fought back, he almost shouted that this urge for violence must have its origins in some Slav cossack. The implication being that the alien genes that had produced a Jew who looked like a cossack had also carried the cossack taste for violence and blood. In the fall I would return to my old school and I would intensify preparations for my bar mitzvah.

My mother considered my entrance into manhood already complete. I needed no ritual in a synagogue to sanctify the fact. But she deferred to my father, agreeing to enroll me in the public school in September.

The day I was to rejoin my long familiar classmates, the German army invaded Poland.

"THE GERMAN ARMY INVADED POLAND."

How removed, how factual that must sound to you. Ancient history. Like the rule of Charlemagne, the German invasion of Poland in 1939 does not

25

concern you. Consider this calendar now that you know your father is (suddenly!) a Jew:

September 1, 1939	Germany invades Poland. World War II begins.
September 27, 1939	Warsaw surrenders.
October 12, 1939	First deportation of Jews from Austria and Moravia to Poland.
October 28, 1939	Jewish star introduced.
November 23, 1939	Identifying armband required of all Jews in central Poland.
October 2, 1940	Order for the creation of the Warsaw ghetto.
November 15, 1940	The Warsaw ghetto is sealed off.
July 22, 1942	Warsaw "resettlement" begins. Transportation to the Belzec and Treblinka concentration camps begins.
April 19, 1943	Uprising of the Warsaw ghetto.
May 16, 1943	Warsaw ghetto destroyed.
August 2, 1943	Uprising in Treblinka.

26

I hope that after you read these pages I have written, "The German army invaded Poland" does not seem an ancient, removed fact.

It is difficult, from this distance of over thirty years, to reconstruct those days following the invasion. But one word bumps me into another word that guides me into a memory hooked to other memories.

An example: a walk my father and I took on September 29, two days after Warsaw surrendered. We were on our way to visit Grandmother, to be sure she was not hurt. There were no buses, of course, so we walked. For almost two hours.

Great piles of burning debris filled streets and sidewalks. All utilities had been destroyed. Repairs lasted for a few hours and then the utilities failed again. People were waiting in long lines to reach the banks of the Vistula, where they could dip their buckets and carry water home. The water could not be boiled because there was no fuel. Knowing that an epidemic would not be selective, the Germans ordered the dead bodies in the streets to be buried in the city squares and public gardens. I had never seen a dead body before. Now I saw hundreds.

Because Grandmother's apartment house in the

Krasinski Gardens had received little damage from German bombs or troops, and because our house had no roof, we agreed that we would all be safer and more comfortable living together in Grandmother's apartment. After all, it would only be for a short time.

We lived together for over a year, grateful that all the tenants in Grandmother's apartment house were old friends of hers, Gentiles who loved her. Whenever we went outside, which we rarely did, we had to identify ourselves as Jews. The law was specific:

> The identification is to take the form of an armband, to be worn on the upper arm of clothing and outer clothing, bearing on its outer side a blue Star of David against a white background. The white background must be at least 10 cm. wide. The star must be of such a size that there is at least 8 cm. between the opposite points of the star. The lines forming the star must be at least 1 cm. wide.

More and more refugees were swarming into the city of Warsaw, hoping to find safety among the population already there, or at least anonymity. Perhaps even peace.

Long before I had been born, there had been a Jewish institution in Warsaw known as the Kehilla. The Germans revived the Council of the Kehilla and gave it the name of *der Judenrat.* It was not religious; it was racial, with jurisdiction over all matters affecting the Jewish "race."

Led by Adam Cherniakow, a member of the old Kehilla Council, the Judenrat was composed of twenty-four Jewish members. Its duties were to register all Jews: issue birth certificates, business licenses, and permits; collect government taxes from Jews; issue ration cards and collect payments for them; and register workers. The registered workers supplied the Germans with their slave labor.

My father went out every night to meet with groups of Jews who debated the wisdom of obeying the German orders as processed through the Kehilla. The majority of the Kehilla Council argued that the German organization of forced labor would be a deterrent to the many gangs of Polish thugs roaming the streets, seizing Jews and delivering them to the German work gangs. Cherniakow and the others had promised to be fair, to select men in rotation so that no single man or family would suffer more than the others, but the procedure became, in its own way, as evil as the Germans'. Rich Jews often paid high fees to be exempt from forced labor. The result: the battalions of Jewish laborers were staffed almost exclusively by the poor.

On October 2, 1940, the Germans ordered the creation of the Warsaw ghetto. All Jews living in predominantly Gentile neighborhoods were to move to the ghetto. All non-Jews living in what was to be the ghetto were to leave by October 31. Just before that deadline, the Germans extended the date to November 15, and on November 15 the ghetto was sealed off. Not wanting to put the goodwill of Grandmother's tenant neighbors to further test, Mother and Father, after long discussions with Grandmother, decided that Grandmother and Sonia would not be safe if the three of us stayed with them any longer. I, a boy, and much older than Sonia, could endure whatever rigors the ghetto might bring. When this war was over, we assured each other, we would all leave Poland together, the five of us. We had relatives in Paris, in London, somewhere in the United States.

Intent on not attracting attention to the apartment window, through which Grandmother and Sonia were watching Mother, Father, and me walk down

Swietojerska Street—and, I am sure, waving to us—
we did not look back. If anything changed my father,
it was that. That forced separation, that merciless
farewell. He was convinced, I think, that he would
never see his baby daughter again. My mother, aware
of his pain, as if she bore none herself, reached over
to take the heavy suitcase he was carrying. He shook
his head and trudged on.

In the ghetto, each Jew was alloted a very small
ration of food. As a result, the Jewish food industry
was virtually destroyed. With no market, no poultry
or meat or fish to buy or sell, the butchers, like
everyone else, spent their days and nights hiding in
their freezing apartments. If they were fortunate
enough to have or share an apartment.

The Germans prohibited the production of shoes,
clothing, textiles, and metal goods intended for sale
to Jews. So Jewish men, who had relied on Jews
to buy their products, wandered the streets of the
ghetto or huddled together in dark rooms, free to
be grabbed and rushed off to work in German factories and fields.

But ingenuity bloomed. Former shoemakers began
producing shoes with fabric tops and wooden soles.
Tailors patched and reweaved, reversing suits and

shirts and coats so that, sewn inside out, they might appear less shabby.

Many Polish peasants and workers, unable to earn enough money from the Germans, turned to smuggling into the ghetto whatever might be of value to the Jews. Chicken, fish, beef found their way through, over, or under the walls. Enough to generate a number of small illegal slaughterhouses. Factories, also illegal and well concealed, rendered surplus animal fat into soap and candles as well as barely usable fuel. Because sugar had disappeared from every table, except those occupied by German soldiers, an illegal and concealed saccharin industry catered to Jews who had a sweet tooth and zlotys to spare.

Tobacco was in heavy demand. Polish workers in tobacco factories sold enough stolen leaf to the Jews to support a fair number of Jewish workers in the curing and shredding of tobacco and the manufacture of cigarettes. To extend the supply of tobacco, it was often mixed—too often, too liberally—with beet leaves.

When the streets were thought clear of German soldiers, men and women and children hunted through ruined buildings for rags, paper, glass, tin. Broken windows in the apartments were either covered with wood or heavy paper or fitted with large panes of glass produced by piecing together fragments from shattered windows. As substitutes for electricity or gas, homemade calcium carbide lamps produced enough light so children were not compelled to go to sleep at dusk. They could sit up and study as long as they wished.

The streets were filled with corpses covered with newspapers. In the morning, I would hear on every street corner the weak voices of starving men or women or children. In the evening, on every street corner, several of those beggars would be lying in the gutter, dead.

The reception centers for refugees were openly referred to as Death Centers. Typhus patients, panicked by the corpses around them, fled into the streets from their rooms, their bodies ravaged by the disease as well as by starvation. The poor dragged their dead relatives to the streets during the night to escape the payment of twenty zlotys to an undertaker. Unrecorded, the death did not have to be reported. With the death unreported, the ration card would continue to be active.

In the midst of such depravity, my mother and father managed somehow to remain not only humane but selfless. All that had composed their world before their arrival in the ghetto was cast aside, forgotten. The moment, the present, was important only in how it might affect the future. They, and many others, were truly heroic, building and maintaining not just courage and pride but an awareness of history, of their own history.

Unfortunately for me—and I realized this gradually—I was no longer the center of their universe. Something larger than I, than my own life, took precedence. Jews, Jewishness, Judaism obsessed them. As if a trumpet call issued in the days of Abraham, Isaac, and Jacob was only now making itself heard, only now sounding at this time in this place. As German brutality increased, the struggle to survive intensified. The more the Germans defiled the word *Jew,* the more intent were the Jews to give it holy honor.

During those days and nights I would lie on the roofs and try to recall forgotten prayers that would, I hoped, once again connect my mother and father to me.

4

From early morning until late at night, my mother and father participated in almost every organization that existed in the ghetto.

TOZ, the organization for Jewish health, distributed vaccines and worked to improve the hygiene in every part of the ghetto, setting up clinics, children's homes, communal kitchens, public baths. Another organization, Centos, cared for children whose parents had been sent to labor camps. It also contributed to the Jewish Children's Hospital, supported homes for deaf children and children of refugees, and organized day camps in dirt lots strewn with the rubble of war.

35

Various political and social and labor organizations established primitive soup kitchens or tearooms for their members and sympathizers. There the latest events, the differing theories, could be discussed.

All the organizations, regardless of their religious or political orientation, relied on one particular source for funds as well as physical and moral support. That was the Joint Distribution Committee, which continued to receive money almost exclusively from American Jews, rich and poor. The JDC provided funds for TOZ (medical and hygiene), for Centos (aid for the poor and orphaned and handicapped children), and ORT (trade schools and training centers). Throughout the ghetto the JDC soup kitchens, crowded as they were, accepted every new arrival.

Members of the Labor Bund, which was the General Jewish Socialist Labor Union, operated two mimeograph machines. The members had different talents and responsibilities, and did not work in the same buildings so that should some of the people be captured by the Germans, other comrades would not be in danger.

Workers also set up the Socialist Red Cross, which was divided into three sections, one of which cared for the needy and the sick, organized medical aid, procured virtually nonexistent drugs, and made food and clothing collections. A second section located hiding places and cared for comrades certain to be executed if captured. A third section provided food and clothing for those who were arrested or who were in labor camps, and maintained contact with the prisoners.

And so, Maggie—and Karin and Birte and Jon— it must appear to you that that life was not so bad. After all, with so many organizations caring for us, we Jews must have been able to endure Polish and German treatment with fair comfort and security. Unfortunately, the successes described here proved to be no more significant than a ripple in the Atlantic Ocean. Jews of all ages succumbed to disease and depression.

As hunger and typhus destroyed Jews inside the ghetto, the labor camps took their toll outside. What the long hours of labor did not accomplish, the Ukrainian and Lithuanian guards did. Labor-camp survivors returned to the ghetto weak and sick, mutilated, feet wrapped in rags, often dressed only in their underwear and sometimes not even in that. A few days after their return to the ghetto, the same men would be herded together again and carried off to the *Umschlagplatz.*

Before the decree of November 15 that denied non-Jews entry to the ghetto, many Polish Gentiles risked their lives to visit their Jewish friends, bringing clothing and food (of which they themselves had precious little), sometimes even medicines or money or tobacco, but always sympathy and support. Protestant and Catholic, they were well aware of the hazards, but they came.

The Kasinskis, who had visited us twice since our arrival in the ghetto, visited us for the last time on Wednesday. Roman Kasinski worked for the same publishing house for which my father had worked. They had shared offices and problems for thirty years. Anya Kasinski and my mother had been as close as sisters. Julie and Sophie, twins born two days after I was born, had been in love with me, and I with them, ever since our mothers had first pushed our prams through the parks. We had promised that when we grew up, I would marry both Julie and Sophie, and we would live together and love each other forever.

Late Wednesday afternoon, as the Kasinskis prepared to leave, everyone was weeping. Without speaking of it, we knew we'd probably never see each other again. I hugged Julie and Sophie. We walked the Kasinskis to the gate. I heard a few guarded remarks about Grandmother, about Sonia. I heard Grandmother's address repeated. Embraces again. And tears.

Nineteeen months later, on June 23, 1942, Anya and Sophie were among the first group selected for extinction in the gas chamber at Auschwitz. Polish neighbors had informed the Gestapo that the Kasinskis had had close Jewish friends and had even visited them in the ghetto. Roman Kasinski died October 14, 1943, at the concentration camp of Sobibor, when he led an uprising. Julie had been shopping when the Gestapo came for the family. She is alive now, in an institution for the insane in Warsaw.

Partly to keep her sanity, partly out of love and devotion, Mother went to work in an orphanage run by Dr. Janusz Korczak, a famous writer and educator. So she and my father were gone from our apartment all day, every day. They assured each other, and me, that I would be protected by one of the many relatives with whom we shared the apartment. They did not know that I was using tricks and excuses to escape to the streets every day. The relatives, preoccupied with their own survival and reassured by my safe return every evening, saw no need to inform my parents that I too was gone.

One afternoon in December or January—I recall a cold wind—I was striding down Zamenhofa when a hand gripped my shoulder. I prepared to leap free and dash through the streets, but the voice was familiar. I looked up. There stood my father, eyes angry, face dark. After a few stern words and a lecture that in less than a minute dropped from threatening to endearing, he took my hand and walked with me along the street. "Come," he said. "We must be kind to each other. Shall we hear some music?"

I knew there were cafes in the ghetto where Jews could hear poets and musicians and see plays performed. In the midst of this depravity there were several theaters offering performances in both Polish and Yiddish.

We went to a cafe—sticky counters, broken chairs, lukewarm drinks of some clear liquid that bore just a hint of a fruit flavor. My father and I sat there, close together, among the starving, the sick, the near mad, who still knew the need, often paying with their last zlotys, to hear Szlengel read his poetry or Marysia Ajzensztat, "the nightingale of the ghetto," sing her songs.

When Ajzensztat sang the Yiddish lament "Eli, Eli," wailing and weeping filled the air at the words "Save me, save me, from danger." At "My God, my God, why hast Thou forsaken us," my father clutched my arm with one hand and buried his face in the other hand.

I roamed the roofs of the ghetto.

Ever since November, when we'd arrived, I'd spent many days, sometimes with friends but mostly alone, exploring the roof world. As if I had a prophetic sense of the role those roofs would one day play in my life. The roofs were like books I had to read and, in time, be tested on.

I remember one such evening, a Monday, when from one of the roofs, I saw my mother below on the street, walking home. She had been with Dr. Korczak all day. She seemed more exhausted than she usually was. Every few minutes she stopped, as if to rest. Her head tilted back and she took deep breaths.

When I arrived at the apartment, she was sitting on a stool, staring into space. She seemed oblivious to my hugs, my kisses. My father, fortunately, had returned early from a meeting of the Defense Committee. He had made tea for my mother, and when

41

I entered, he was wrapping her in extra coats and rubbing her hands. Aunts and uncles, bustling about, trying to help, bumped and pushed me out of the way. I watched from a corner of the room. My mother's famous beauty, her youthful resilience, were gone. Since this morning, it seemed to me, her hair had turned not gray but white.

Eventually, after more hot tea, more solace, more prodding, she was able to tell us what had happened. That afternoon there had been a funeral in another orphanage. Twelve children had died of hunger. The children in my mother's orphanage had sent a wreath accompanied by a message: *From children who are starving to children who have died of starvation.*

That night I lay silent under my coats, unable to sleep. I was fighting against a rising wave of pity for those children, for all children in the ghetto. As if pity might weaken my resolve to survive. I knew I should be nursing a hatred for the Germans, nursing it and letting it flourish; I knew I should let what was an almost vague promise of vengeance grow into an intense vow. But I felt nothing. Numbness hovered inside my body, just beneath my skin. Seeping inward, it seemed to evolve into a sorrow so intense that nothing, certainly not weeping, would ease it. And then what had been sorrow was suddenly replaced by loathing, a loathing that had no direction and no specific target. In the darkness, alone in the midst of warm human bodies, I loathed not just the Germans but the Jews too, Mother and Father, all things human. Why I didn't leave the room and climb to the roof and leap to the cobblestoned street, I'll never know.

In all the years that followed that night—even during the ghetto uprising and then during the weeks at Treblinka—I never again reached such appalling depths. Surviving that night must have fueled my confidence that I could survive forever.

5

I was in the streets all day, every day, even in the freezing weather of January and February. I saw and heard everything, and remembered details that could be of use. My mind worked like a computer during those last months of 1940 and the early months of 1941. What might contribute to my survival arsenal was stored; what had no use was rejected. What was stored established a connection to muscles and nerves. I learned how to shuffle in submission, how to swagger like a Polish thug. I could run for hours without rest. I could scramble like a monkey across ropes or narrow catwalks on

44

steep roofs. I acquired almost an animal ability to fade into backgrounds, melt into shadows. And, as I said on the first page of this . . . shall I call it a book? . . . there was luck. Luck served me so well, so often, that I was convinced I had a charmed life. That security led to brazen feats that others would have considered suicidal to try. I was invulnerable.

But I was still human.

Sometimes, especially during the freezing winter or the spring rains, when I would hurry along the Karmelicka or through the Zamenhofa Nalewki quarter—the so-called Little Ghetto—and pass the people begging in the streets, my sense of invulnerability would be tested. What had decided that I should not be one of those starving beggars? What had decided that they should not have the capacities for survival?

Late at night, even after curfew, when the streets were almost silent, the pleas from the starving carried in harsh whispers through the darkness. *"Yiddische kinder, git a shtikl broit."* Jews, give us a piece of bread. Small children in rags might sob for an hour or two, but by early morning they would be corpses on the streets and sidewalks. Apartment walls contained posters proclaiming Children's Month or Our

Children Must Not Die! or Children Are Sacred! How many times, day and night, I saw the corpses of children covered with those posters.

How did I keep from going mad, from dying? *Survive, Gideon . . . at any cost . . .*

November, 1941. Enough. I had to get out of the ghetto.

My first escape was almost exactly one year after we'd moved there. I was ready but I was also frightened. I was thirteen.

Morning. I silently followed a fourteen-year-old girl named Esther. She had been slipping through the wall for months and, in the evenings, returning with food for her family. I followed her, copying her every act, every gesture, until she stopped and chased me, demanding I follow her no longer. Alone, frightened, I stayed far behind, until I saw her approach a German soldier and accompany him into an apartment house.

Esther never returned to the ghetto.

From that day on I left the ghetto every day. When I was captured and taken to the *Umschlagplatz,* and escaped, I had already been visiting Aryan Warsaw for about eight months. Yankele and I had been together for five of those eight, and I had been with One-Eye and the gang the last three.

We moved many times after our arrival. How many, I can't remember. I have forgotten the addresses. I know that the last place we lived was an apartment on Nowolipki. That was where I returned the day I escaped from the train.

By the time we moved to Nowolipki, every street corner had its patrols. The Germans, in their long stone-gray coats and steel helmets, were indifferent to all others, foe or friend. There were Polish policemen, known in the ghetto as the Blues because of the color of their uniforms. The *Jüdischer Ordnungsdienst,* the Jewish police, in their jackboots and black caps, always stood apart from both the Germans and the Blues. White bands on their arms bore the Star of David. They received a few extra zlotys as well as extra rations and a promise of security if, and only if, they proved capable of disciplining their Jewish brothers and sisters. To keep themselves and their families, they not only proved capable, they often proved as vicious and thorough as the Germans, the Ukrainians, and the Lithuanians the Germans hired to do their dirtiest work. The Jewish police were condemned by most Jews, were always hated. But cruel as they were, and unreliable, they were occasionally capable of minimal charity, their guilt occasionally vulnerable to exploitation.

At the gates in the ghetto walls, the guards were always German. Such passageways could not be trusted to Blues or the Jews. But even the Germans were open to trickery and, almost as often, to bribery. When escaping through walls or through tunnels or under carriages or in trucks was not possible, I had no choice but to use the gates. The opportunities came faster and easier on some days than on others. Occasionally I had to wait for hours for a familiar guard, or at least a guard who might be approachable. At other times the guards were distracted enough for someone such as I, someone alert and cunning (and, I must admit, someone possessing a cold and unyielding heart), to glide out or in through the gate.

An illustration: an incident that took place, I'd guess, about two months after that message from the starving orphans.

A column of Jews (all men) marched out of the Aryan sector. They carried canvas bags, battered suitcases, bundles tied with ropes. A contingent of Blues led the way. The German soldiers at the gate stepped back, as if both the Blues and the Jews had a common contagious disease. The Jews, tired and dirty, bared their heads as was required. One of the younger men, eyes glazed, failed to remove his hat. A German soldier shouted, stopped the marching unit, and ordered the Blues to drag out the guilty prisoner. The young man seemed unaware of his surroundings as he was pulled and jerked and thrown to the ground. He continued muttering in an incoherent monotone. Praying. He neither groaned nor complained when a Blue's jackboot found his ribs. The German soldier shouted and his comrades laughed, urging him on. The shout brought six Jewish policemen from the opposite side of the street. The German gave an order. The Jewish police hesitated, but when the order was repeated and the German drew his Luger, the six Jewish policemen opened their trousers and urinated on the young man. The comrades of the German soldier applauded. After the Blues marched off the rest of the prisoners, with the Jewish policemen following, the man on the ground sat up. The German shot twice. The man dropped back and lay still. The soldier and his comrades gathered again at the gate to smoke and laugh.

I, in the meantime, was well on my way.

While the Germans had been enjoying their little game, two streetcars coming from Aryan Warsaw and Krasinski Gardens had passed through the gate. I'd nonchalantly climbed aboard the platform of the last car. On the platform, watching the event, was a Blue. It was his duty to prohibit anyone from boarding the streetcar on its way through the ghetto. We watched the final moments and the shooting together. The Polish Blue was so intent on the scene that he did not see me. Or pretended not to. His back was turned, and his hands were clasped together behind his trousers, fingers extended. Thanks to previous escapades, previous contacts with guards and streetcar workers, I knew what to do. The zlotys fit the cavity formed by his fingers perfectly. I strolled past him and into the car.

All the passengers were Poles who, in order to move from one area of the city to another, had no choice but to use the train. They paid no attention to me as I searched for an empty seat. Passengers were often stepping to the platform for a breath of air and returning. And after all, with my blond hair and blue eyes and easy manner, I could only be a Pole, one of them.

I had been very frightened the first time I pushed my way onto a streetcar, my pockets stuffed with a tattered collection of scarves and gloves. But each new success permitted me to buy items of better quality and greater utility. My self-assurance intensified, I swaggered like a young Polish thug and even created a certain sullen sneer that convinced both Poles and Germans. Now and then, in the ghetto, I'd forget where I was, and I'd see the Jews back away and cringe, and then I'd have to convert before their eyes, speaking Yiddish or Hebrew with the familiar Warsaw accent.

At times, if I weakened and felt nostalgia or sentimentality approaching, I recalled early childhood joys with my mother and father. I felt so old, so estranged, and I longed for my young, innocent self. I yearned for that ancient time when I'd not had to think about being a Jew, when I'd not been reminded every day, every hour, every minute, that I was a Jew. I frequently turned familiar corners and half expected to see myself and Julie and Sophie Kasinski playing in the Krasinski Gardens, to see myself with my father, leaving that pastry shop on Jerusalem Avenue.

I could not let myself dwell on such memories. The next step would be a questioning of the present, callous Gideon. I always succeeded in diverting or putting off such memories by reminding myself that I had appointments, that there was work to do. One-Eye and my gang were waiting.

The evening One-Eye and his gang first approached me on Dluga Street, I thought my end had come. Filthy, drunk, hateful, they grabbed me not because I was a Jew (they did not know that yet) but because I was an outsider invading their turf. They punched me, pushed me into an alley, knocked me down, took my zlotys, and removed my shoes. The one whose feet the shoes fit best took them with him. They left me alive, thanks to my papers that proved I was a Gentile.

Those papers and the travel pass had saved my life before and were to save it again. According to those papers, I was a young Pole living on the Aryan side of the wall. To enhance that image, I wore a silver chain around my neck with, open to view, a silver medal of the Virgin Mary. I had memorized certain prayers and catch phrases in Polish and Latin, so that if I were captured and questioned, I could prove my Catholic heritage.

I was always afraid I would forget to remove the chain before I joined my parents each evening, but so far they were unaware of my disguise.

The members of that gang were probably the worst thugs in Warsaw. They competed with each other to demonstrate their contempt for both life and death. Their risks were much like my own. If they were apprehended, their punishment would be the same as mine. Beatings, a labor camp, death. They could not be less concerned. They existed only to enjoy vast amounts of vodka, vast amounts of food, and vast amounts of women. On those infrequent days when funds were low, they roamed the streets in search of Jews. Capture of Jews and delivery of them to the SS or the Gestapo meant significant spending money.

There were five more difficult encounters after that first one. Seeking food or clothes or medicine or tobacco to take back to the ghetto, or, more important, seeking liasons who would be willing to divert large amounts of such material to the ghetto (for a price) took me into all areas of Aryan Warsaw. It also earned me additional attention from One-Eye and his gang. My value to the gang grew in direct proportion to the growth in value of what I carried in my sacks and pockets. They indulged me now and then, pushing me rather than punching me, talking to me rather than hurling epithets. Why destroy the Santa Claus who brings you free gifts? Just knock him around a bit, enough to let him know you're in control.

My sixth meeting with the gang was decisive. Before they could touch me, I reached into my sack and pulled out a large bottle of vodka. I opened it. "Here, there's more where this came from. Free. Only I know where it comes from and how to get it."

They'd been drinking but weren't drunk enough yet to be dangerous. They were so astonished by what looked like lack of fear that they considered the offer seriously. And in mild shock. We went to a cellar that was part bar, part cafe, part toilet. They began to relax. By now there was a mild familiarity among us. After all, if you beat someone often enough and he returns smiling, offering you vodka, and appearing to bear no grudges, what else can you do but relax and try to understand him?

I had to work fast, to trap them before their mood turned ugly, fueled by the vodka. "I want to talk business. I am a Jew."

Counting One-Eye, there were five of them. For a moment they sat like five pieces of gray granite sculpture. No one could believe what they'd heard, if they'd heard it. "I'm a Jew," I repeated.

A Jew, outside the ghetto, knowing there was a

price on his head, was freely admitting the fact to these Gentile Jew-traders. I was not only defying the Germans and them, I was obviously succeeding financially. More, obviously, than they were. I'd returned after many beatings, I'd had my money taken each time, as well as whatever booty I was carrying, and I was now sitting there unconcerned. Most shocking of all, I was suggesting that I be accepted as their equal. I was expecting them to make some business deal.

The largest of the gang had an empty socket where his right eye should have been. He was smiling now. "A little Jew," he said.

The momentum had to be kept up, the important word *profit* repeated. Their grudging respect and attention might waiver and decline at any moment. I promised profits, guaranteed them, for everyone. I would do most of the dirty work, I would take the major risks, but the profits would be shared equally. And profits there would be. Plenty of profits. Profits profits profits.

The centuries-old mythology of the shrewd money-grubbing Jew was having its effect, working to my benefit. They were tempted. But shaped by that mythology, they were finding it difficult to free themselves of their suspicion and hatred of Jews.

A young tough, younger even than I, whose face was pockmarked by old boils and sprouting new ones, gave my shoulder a push. Why form a partnership when they could take anything they wanted to take?

I nodded, granting him fine insight. But, I said, what if I were to stop coming to this section of the city? Fewer Jews were alive in the ghetto every day, fewer of those who were alive were daring to leave the ghetto, and fewer of those leaving would engage in smuggling. Soon smuggling would be a rare, even an extinct business. But OK, if they didn't want to make a deal, fine. There were other gangs all over the city.

"Jew," a skinny blond said, "we hand you over to the Germans, we get vodka."

His long, greasy hair soaked a sickly yellow forehead. He was quite drunk, with slurred speech. I was sure the yellow tint in his eyes came not from alcohol but from some disease. I was careful not to drink from his glass.

"You turn me over to the Germans, you get vodka. Once. You don't turn me over and we form this partnership, you'll have more vodka than you can drink. Every day."

That one, I thought, as he dug beneath his fingernails with a long switchblade knife, was dangerous.

One of those Poles who for centuries had not just supported pogroms but provoked them. Participated in them.

It was because of the Jews, he went on, that the Germans were here. Good. Let the Germans collect Poland's garbage.

Because the others were older—sixteen or seventeen—they were, perhaps, wiser. At least they were more realistic. There is a time for honesty and there is a time for business. My ordering a second bottle of vodka gave me a chance to flash a fistful of money, an appetizer for the feast that I, and only I, could serve. If they were sensible. Hatred? Was hatred very profitable these days? No. But this little Jew was. Or could be.

I did not deceive myself. I could almost read their thoughts. For the moment, I could gain them all sorts of luxuries; but when that moment was passed and I was no longer useful, well, my body could still bring them five bottles of vodka.

They were all looking to One-Eye now. Everything had been said. He was their leader, natural or elected. "What sort of partnership?"

I knew I had them.

Instead of beating me, I explained, they would be my protectors. Sometimes they would help me transport the material—whatever was being smuggled into the ghetto—and sometimes they would be my protectors, guarding me if other gangs intervened. As Poles, they could pass through the ghetto on streetcars without risk, so occasionally they would help transfer the collected material to the Jewish porters waiting at their designated stations. I would arrange the many assorted payoffs to all involved officials among the Blues, the Jews, and the Germans. There were still enough Jews with money available to pay for food and clothing and—here I shrugged and shaped a woman's body in the air with my hands—whatever else was required. I fed their appetite for the myth, that famous ever-wealthy Jew.

Was it a deal?

Their delay was for theatrical effect, but I knew how to be theatrical too. I was fourteen, already an experienced producer and director and actor in my own species of theater. I shrugged, started to rise, suggesting there were others who would be interested.

"A deal," One-Eye said. "I trust this little Jew. I almost like him." The others, even Greasehead, nodded.

Another bottle. We drank to the partnership. Not used to consuming such quantities of vodka, I was quite drunk, but not so drunk as to miss the point that my being a Jew was less important than my being a source of vodka. And money.

We all drank ourselves into a stupor. I slept in the bar that night and left early the next morning.

It was early, but the cafes on Nowy Swiat were filling up with strolling Germans and Polish women who were finding the presence of the Germans in their homeland quite beneficial. As I walked I swaggered, filled with that buoyant assurance that comes when you know you have just proven your superiority over someone bigger and stronger but less cunning than yourself.

There was a pastry shop on Jerusalem Avenue where once my father and I used to buy cakes for the family. (I especially remember now a long chocolate-covered cream-filled delicacy we always treated ourselves to as we walked, my father carrying an extra one for Sonia.) I bought two dozen of the richest and most expensive pastries. Three of them were lost to the conductor on the streetcar, and four more, plus two hundred zlotys, to the German guard at the gate, a fresh-faced boy from Bavaria, who reminisced about eating such pastries at home.

In the ghetto I dropped sixteen into the outstretched hands of sixteen of the starving children haunting the shadows. I saved one for Yankele. We would celebrate our newly organized corporation.

"You take chances," Yankele said. "Tell me, why do you trust them?"

"They think a Jew is sure to get them money. In this case they're right. As long as I do, I'm safe. They need me; we can use them."

"One betrayal from them"—and Yankele drew his finger (which appeared to be almost the size of my wrist) across his throat—"everything will be ruined. Including you." He glared at me. I thought he was going to throw me out of the room or end our partnership or both. Then he rolled his massive shoulders and grinned. "But a hundred other things wait to ruin us. So we're a corporation, eh? Like Krupp or Ford or the Bank of England. We've got offices everywhere. All right. You trust your intuitions. So do I."

6

The German army, as efficient and as powerful as it was, could not control the activities of a half-million people, could not always know where each person was or what he was doing. Nor was the extermination proving to be as simple as had been predicted by their experts. Bodies had to be disposed of, epidemics held at bay, evidence concealed from the world's probing eyes. The extermination process contained its own built-in controls. For the moment.

As long as the Jews were alive, they had to be utilized. Collecting them from the streets or tearing them out of their rooms, the Germans threw the Jews into shops hastily opened at the edge of the ghetto. There, uniforms and helmets and belts and boots and holsters were produced for the German armed forces, the Wehrmacht.

Of every hundred items produced, at least ten found their way into the hands of the new Yankele–Gideon–One-Eye corporation.

Yankele was not at all upset by the comments of the members of the gang. They didn't want to deal directly with the Jewish porters: fine. If they ever changed their minds, also fine. Each side needed the other, and as long as his porters didn't lose anything, the Poles could act however they wished.

To see Yankele—this human tank, with a face that looked as if tank treads had crossed it not once but several times—work hoists and winches and shoulder heavy bags and boxes, you'd think he was motivated by the promise of great wealth or personal authority. He cared for neither. He worked because he'd worked hard all his life and was not about to let the Germans stop him. He was as courageous as he was strong, though he was always practical. He'd not dare travel to Aryan Warsaw. "With this mug, they wouldn't have to make me drop my pants to find out if I was a Jew. Could this mug belong to an Irishman or a Frenchman?"

What I enjoyed especially, visiting with Yankele

in his warehouse, was the relief from the sense of death and hate that prevailed in the ghetto. Yankele lived to work, to gamble, to smuggle, to outwit authorities and bureaucrats. For Yankele, living in the ghetto was not much different from living in Warsaw or Vilna. He was not impressed with his strength, but he knew when to use it. In peacetime, as part of the Labor Bund, he had been more than willing to use his muscle when the brains of the Bund leaders floundered.

He'd called me to meet him one day after I'd been working the streets of Aryan Warsaw for several months. He needed a young assistant who could act as liaison for him outside the ghetto. I knew the streets; I spoke fluent German; I had proven my talents for smuggling and making money; and best of all, I looked like a Pole.

Within days of that first meeting, we were more than partners. We were close friends. I would sit with him sometimes for hours in his little room beneath the warehouse, and we'd talk about all sorts of things. He liked to hear about the books I'd read, he taught me card games, he asked me to teach him English, he gave me a detailed history of smuggling in the ghetto.

Without leaving his warehouse but by using runners, contacting certain officials who were under obligation to him, he could perform almost miraculous feats of trade. He established a network of contacts that, were it ever needed, could slip me free of danger before I was killed by the Germans.

I grew closer to Yankele than I was to my parents.

There was a group of Jewish thugs at 13 Leszno Street who, with the approval of the Gestapo, would guarantee what they called "protection" to looters and smugglers, for a price. Known simply as The Thirteen, the group was despised by most Jews. My father and his comrades declared that when the time came, the members of The Thirteen should be wiped out before the Germans.

Because One-Eye and his group would not be in alliance with Yankele and the ghetto porters, exchanging boxes and bags and barrels at specified depots, extra protection was necessary for both Poles and Jews. Most of the time this meant buying off attention, distracting willing Blues and Gestapo while business was being conducted.

Yankele knew several of The Thirteen from the old days, the peacetime Warsaw days. He was contemptuous of them now but conceded that their required fees were formalities, merely tokens of recognition, and would be minimal in proportion to profits earned. He met with The Thirteen. Protection was granted.

There were days when the gang and I made ten or twelve trips in and out of the ghetto. At times our runs were so productive that teams of Jewish porters could not keep up with us. Yankele was ecstatic. Every evening when I'd stop at his warehouse room on my way back to our apartment on Nowolipki, he would toast me, confessing that "little Gideon" was the best investment he'd ever made. I always expected the glass to be crushed in his hand. It seemed so small and fragile. He assured me several times that when he died, before or after the Germans left Poland, I would be his heir.

One night, after a particularly hectic and dangerous day in Aryan Warsaw, I sat with Yankele, sharing his vodka. For the first time since we'd been together, he was almost sentimental. When I tried to explain or understand my disinterest in the ghetto commitments of my parents by talking, he held up his hand. His face grew grim, almost severe. "My little Gideon, my innocent little Gideon. No mushy talk about Jews. It's all a big lie, that Chosen People story. Rabbis, priests, preachers, are the really successful crooks in this world. They sell lies and are praised for it. And paid. I make my own world, my own laws. You've read all those books. So tell me, little Gideon, if Jews are God's Chosen People, why is He doing this to them? Me, I'd rather not be chosen. Or at least God ought to give people turns. That would be fair. You know, Catholics chosen this year, Protestants next year, after that the Moslems. And on and on."

"But, Yankele, why are you working so hard being a smuggler?"

He looked at me as if he were thinking I was not as smart as he'd thought I was.

"And all the money. What will you do with it, Yankele?"

"I'll look at it. Count it. Feel it. Like all misers do. You expect me to give it to the Jewish charities? So they can help everyone who doesn't have the courage to take chances or the brain to think of a job? Fat chance, Little Gideon. I live from day to day. I always have. I have a sister, I help her, make sure she doesn't starve out there in the streets. What else is important?"

"But don't you ever wonder about being here? The Germans put you behind walls, beat you, starve—"

66

His hand went up. "The Germans don't touch me. They are paid well not to. Being put here? Out there in Warsaw, if the Germans weren't marching around, I'd live in a little room under a warehouse. I don't feel loyal to Jews or Poles or elephants. I'm for me." He seemed suddenly aware that he was exposing a part of himself he'd always kept concealed. He motioned toward the door. "Go home, get some sleep. Stop asking questions. There aren't enough answers."

When it was necessary for the gang to follow me into the ghetto, they wore Star of David armbands. After the first trip, they were never quite the same. Not even Greasehead.

They stared at the corpses in the street. Corpses in streets were no novelty to them. But most of these corpses were children. Often babies. The beggars in the streets were not only men and women, but included boys and girls wrapped in layers of rags.

Once, when One-Eye slipped a few zlotys into the hands of a yellow-skinned girl, she fell over dead as her fingers closed on his own.

On our third trip into the ghetto, about a month after we began working together, I had to rush the gang into hiding. The Germans had begun an *Ak-*

tion—a sudden sweep through the streets.

We waited four hours in a cellar, and then, when the Germans came near, we scurried through a tunnel that ended up in a house in the Aryan side of the wall. We went up to the attic, which was concealed by a door with a lavatory fixed to it. From the attic we all watched through cracks between the boards covering the windows as Polish Blues and Ukrainians chased a family out of their apartment and shot them all in the street.

When I considered it safe, I suggested we leave the house. One-Eye reached out a foot and nudged Greasehead. "Hey, Andrzej, you like the way the Germans collect our Polish garbage?"

Greasehead shrugged and made a face that implied disinterest. But he snapped his switchblade closed and stood up, muttering a curse that included the words *German pigs*.

My rapport with One-Eye and the gang continued to improve. The gang recognized me as indispensable to their new and growing wealth, and paid me a respect that was no longer forced or reluctant. They no longer considered me a Jew weakling, a Jew who hid from danger, a Jew who paid others to do his nasty jobs. I was still "the little Jew," but now there was an added adjective. I was "the tough little Jew."

When I mentioned this to Yankele, he hugged me with one arm and lifted me about three feet off the ground. "Tough little Jew! Ha! You aren't so tough. You still worry deep down why you aren't *a good Jew* fighting to protect King Saul and King David. Yeah? Am I right?"

I often left our apartment before anyone was awake, and I returned after everyone was asleep. Now and then I brought a revolver for my father's growing resistance army, sometimes pieces of a rifle or a machine gun that could be joined to other pieces delivered earlier. More often I brought money with which my father's fighters could buy what they needed, if what they needed was available.

My father always accepted what I brought, but he rarely said more than "Good" or "We need this, yes." He never asked how or where I obtained what I gave him. Occasionally he seemed almost annoyed at himself for accepting what I offered, but he always accepted it. I told myself his manner came from his fatigue, his depression, his preoccupation with larger, more important things than recognizing little gifts from his son.

I rarely saw my mother. She often stayed at the

orphanage for days on end. When I did see her, she was not apologetic, she was matter-of-fact about her absence. Those were children who had no one to love them, no one to assure them; they had to be protected. Right up to the end. That phrase—*right up to the end*—occurred several times, but I ignored its implications. She too was exhausted.

Each night I returned to the ghetto I brought a pocketful of bread or fruit or a few precious eggs and even, occasionally, cakes or candies. These I doled out to the unbelieving lumps of rags on the sidewalks. I will not forget—this I used to dream about a lot, Maggie, and I know you must have wondered, but you never said a word—the evening I placed a cream-filled pastry in a child's mouth and stood there patiently as the child slowly chewed and swallowed and then regurgitated the entire pastry. The stomach rejected such riches. But bending over, face on the ground, the child tried again.

Every Friday night, after the sad efforts to celebrate the Sabbath, I delivered equal shares of cash to each of the organizations striving to protect those Jews not yet dead. I never thought much about it at the time. I wasn't driven to be charitable with my earnings. I didn't have a hope or a belief that anything I or anyone else did could change things. I simply had more money than I could spend, and had to do something with it.

Once, when Yankele asked me about my plans, I laughed. Plans? Who could make plans? Didn't everyone live from day to day? He was a bit embarrassed to have his own words thrown back at him, but he finally laughed and rubbed my head. I asked him—why, I don't know, I'd not been considering the plan at all—I asked him if he could guess how much it would take to bribe all the required officials to get me out of the ghetto, out of Poland, out of Europe. After all, if he and the past year had taught me anything, it was that everything, everyone, had a price.

Where would I go? Yankele asked.

He was considering the question with such seriousness that his gargoyle face, grotesquely contorted in thought, appeared more human than it ever had. I wondered why he thought the way he did. But he'd asked me a question. Where would I go?

I would go to London, I replied. America, maybe. Yes, America.

Yankele considered me for a moment, and for the first—and only—time, he came to me and swept me into his massive body. Then, with a gentle thrust, he pushed me away. "Little Gideon, there are not enough zlotys in all of Poland."

In his own rough way Yankele loved me as my mother and father would have, had they not been caught up in the ghetto struggles. Gruff, always cynical, but never hateful. He could not hate even the Germans. He certainly could not hate One-Eye, with whom he spent many hours perfecting techniques by which they could communicate with each other should there be a crisis, especially a crisis which could include the capture of "Little Gideon." These discussions always took place in the warehouse cellar because it was far easier for One-Eye to move in and out of the ghetto than it would have been for Yankele. Yankele was always reminding me that with his mug he could be identified as nothing but a Jew. "God chose me? He could have chosen to give this mug to One-Eye."

Earlier I told you that certain facts were necessary. What writers, I said, would call flashbacks. You should, I said, know details about the place, about the times, about my parents, your grandparents. Well, that's done now.

In the years since the war, I have almost succeeded

in shoving aside memories of One-Eye and Yankele and all the others. They have almost ceased to exist. Did they ever really exist? Or are they figments of my imagination?

They existed. As I write now, I remember them so distinctly that the pain and the pleasure of our lives seem as intense today as they did then. I wish desperately now that I could have managed to convey to both Yankele and One-Eye my gratitude for their friendship, their trust, their love. I think, as I write, that now that I have permitted myself to remember everything, I might do more, I might go further. Could I, next week, next month, return to Warsaw? Could I search out One-Eye? Is he alive? Ah, what a reunion that could be.

And so I take you back now to that part of the story when I escaped from the train. Note that, without thinking, I called it a "story."

It is after the escape, after my father's killing of the German and the capture of the Luger. After my father's insistence that Yankele will contaminate me. That I too will soon be nothing but a thug, a smuggler.

It is a Thursday night when I hear him weeping, when I take him in my arms. I do not try to convey to him the depth of my love for Yankele. I do not try to inform him of the role I now play in the ghetto's smuggling operations.

Yankele is killed two days later, on a Saturday morning.

The Sabbath means nothing to Yankele. He always works Friday evening and Saturday. So do I, though I always tell my parents I am only going for a morning walk.

At the precise moment agreed upon, and at the precise location agreed upon, a package of silver and gold is hurled over the wall from the Aryan side. It is to be converted into jewelry by the ghetto's finest artisans, former jewelers and gold- and silversmiths. It will be returned to Yankele as rings and bracelets and pendants; he, in turn, will get it back to the Gestapo officer responsible for having this package of precious metal delivered.

In the past when similar packages were hurled over the wall, we—either Yankele or I—would be waiting. This time we are both there. This time the package catches in the barbed wire and glass shards that top the wall.

Yankele throws a grappling hook with attached rope over the top of the wall. The hook catches. I run to climb the rope, but Yankele, with a sharp command, pulls me back. He goes up the rope like a monkey. At the top, clinging to the rope with his left hand, he gropes inside the wire with his right, but he either cannot locate it or cannot loosen it. He stands, crouched, on top of the wall. Several rifles fire at once. Yankele drops on the Aryan side.

A few minutes later the Germans bring his body to the ghetto side of the wall. They prop it up so that his swollen eyes stare straight ahead. A swastika has been painted on his forehead with his own blood. His arms—those huge hairy muscular arms—are wrapped around a piece of heavy paper on which the Germans have written, also in Yankele's blood: JEW BANDITS CANNOT ESCAPE!!!

Two days later his sister delivers a mud-covered metal box to me. A tag on the box has writing on it that has been recently placed there: *For Gideon. For his trip to America.*

7

The night of the day I receive Yankele's box, I return home after not having been there for almost seventy-two hours. I feel my way across the dark room, over and around sleeping bodies, until I locate an available blanket I might slide beneath. Eyes open, I relive the day's crises, hiding and running and escaping as I had hidden and run and escaped—narrowly—all day, in the streets of Aryan Warsaw.

Since Yankele's death, I have been in command of his ring of porters. Me, Gideon, fourteen years old. Fourteen years and four months. I doubt that I weigh a hundred pounds, though lately, with such an abundance of food available to me, I have actually been gaining weight.

I have attained a certain notoriety. Parents consider me a representation of all the evils waiting inside the ghetto to prey on their children. Now and then I worry about how my mother and father feel about me being a smuggler. After the night when my father tried to denounce Yankele, he and I should have gone on to talk about important things that were happening to us, but neither of us was able to take the first step. In the days that follow, we both retreat into silence, a silence that becomes more difficult to break as we see less and less of each other. I fight against blaming them. I try to build a case that will acquit them. Perhaps they have accepted the fact that my survival means their releasing me, their easing discipline, their asking no questions. Something—I cannot understand what it is—something is motivating them that I have not the slightest physical or spiritual connection to.

My father is working for his Defense Committee, trying to rouse the Jews to fight back, still striving to form a reliable cadre for "that inevitable moment," as my father calls it. My mother still works for Dr. Korczak, who continues to expect all his aids to protect and love the children as he does. My mother, like all the others, complies. She is there day and night. She often does not come home for days. I know she loves me and worries about me, but I am one person; I have a living mother and father; I am toughened to the point of total cynicism. In the orphanage are a hundred children, almost all of them younger, much younger, than I, all of them alone and terrified.

She does not escape the effects of such dedication. Her former toughness has evolved into an obsessive tenderness directed no longer at me or my father but at the children. The orphans. They are to be sheltered as much as is humanly possible, for as long as is humanly possible. Up to the very last moment, if necessary.

My father? Like my mother, he has apparently resigned himself to my precocious maturity. I think that during moments of doubt, when he hears gossip about me, he convinces himself that the intelligence and sensitivity he knows I possess will eventually reign supreme. With my heritage, how can I not, eventually, be a man of ideals?

And so, having received Yankele's box and having returned home, I try to force myself to sleep beneath that blanket. But all I can do is to stare into the darkness and relive the day's escapes. I am just falling off to sleep when my mother's voice, near my shoulder, informs me that the Jewish police have been warned about me. Twice that afternoon they have been to the apartment, looking for me. The Jewish police have been advised by the Gestapo that if they fail to turn me over to the Gestapo in one week, the police will be shot instead of me.

"Now what?" my father asks from some distance to my right.

"What do you mean?"

"Your friend, the great Yankele, is dead. What did it get him, that life he led?"

I cap my anger. I have inherited his command, but the porters are uneasy, knowing I am a child. I do not know what to do. And One-Eye. He and the gang are waiting. Because of my inaction, three people in Aryan Warsaw, police who had delivered contraband to a streetcar station, have been apprehended and shot by the Germans. I am already failing Yankele.

"He died rich?"

I breathe heavily, pretending to be asleep.

"The money you receive. What good will that money do you if you are dead?"

No use pretending. "I will survive," I say. "Remember how you have always—"

"You will survive to be a rich smuggler in England or America? I refuse to believe it."

My mother is sobbing. It's a terrible, heartbreaking sound, and I want to hold her, to reassure her. But what can I say? It is too late for pretense.

Through her sobs she manages to ask if I ever see Sonia or Grandmother when I am over there, on the other side of the wall.

No, of course not. I wouldn't go near Swietojerska Street. That would be as dangerous for them as it would for me. I am always careful.

No one talks for a while, and I think it is over. But then my father says she should go ahead, she should say it, she should ask me.

My mother takes a deep breath. One day, she says, when I cross the wall, when I go to Aryan Warsaw, will I take her with me? She must see Sonia. My father cannot risk the trip. His job, with the turn of events here in the ghetto, requires his remaining here. If I don't help her, she will go alone.

"When do you want to go?"

"Very soon. We do not have much time."

What does she mean? Does she know something I do not know?

Yes. There is to be a German *Aktion* soon. A terrible *Aktion*.

I wait.

The Germans are about to round up everybody— every Jew in the ghetto—for removal to Treblinka.

When?

Soon. No one is sure. Three or four days. Maybe five.

I want to say I'll take her tomorrow. Or the next day. But such a job requires much planning. My mother knows nothing about life in the streets. If she tries without me, she'll never reach the apartment.

"I have to make arrangements," I say. "I'll need a great deal of money. All I have. More. For many different people. Guards. Police. Streetcar conductors. Poles, Germans, Jews."

They are silent. Of course they are. They must be shocked to hear their little blue-eyed baby speak so knowingly, so casually, about the grim realities of the world.

Mother's need to see Sonia becomes my need. I haven't thought of my little sister for so long I can barely recall what she looks like. I could die like Yankele at any moment, any day, and never see her again. I ache to see them both, Sonia and my grandmother. I long to be a part of the family again, in a quiet, peaceful apartment.

I will begin preparations the next morning. My Polish gang will help me. I'll guarantee high profits. And then, this will be my last job.

When I describe my plan to One-Eye, he assures me that it is no more difficult than what we've been doing these past three months. There is one special risk: my mother is not used to our life. More than normal precautions will have to be taken. And precautions cost money. Do I have enough? Yes, I have enough. He suggests my mother put up her hair and wear a man's cap. And she should dress like a man.

I insist that everyone—with the exception of those various intermediaries who will be paid as their services are required—everyone be paid prior to the event. It is clear to me that by the time this is over just about all of my savings, and Yankele's, will be gone.

One-Eye knows this. He takes me aside and says that for the other members of the gang, yes, there should be extra money, a bonus; but as for him, well, I should forget it.

He must have influenced the others, perhaps he even spoke to them. When Greasehead and one other member awkwardly and perhaps a bit reluctantly whisper to me that I needn't worry about bonuses, I say all right, but I have to do something special for them. Greasehead suggests an evening at the Britannia. I agree.

"The last supper?" One-Eye asks, grinning.

The distinctions that existed before the war all over the country continue to exist here in the ghetto. There were always class differences. There had always been rich and poor Jews, with the vast majority poor. There had always been intellectuals and workers. The rich who ended up in the ghetto usually managed to bring a fair portion of their wealth with them, in the form of furs or jewelry or foreign currency or zlotys. They formed exclusive little groups, reassuring each other that the current crisis would be temporary and they would soon be back in business in Warsaw. While they were in the ghetto, available comforts and privileges were to be their due. For some time now, they had remained better off than the mass of Jews; but "better off" meant little. If they had pasted their currencies and their furs at every crack in the window, they still could not have kept out the pervasive odor of decaying corpses.

There are cafes and nightclubs in the ghetto, filled with Jewish police, with the Blues, and with Germans, but filled mostly with the Jews who have clung to their wealth. One store has a display of fine foods in its windows. A cafe exudes the aromas of gourmet dishes.

Representatives from various committees plead with the owners of the cafes and stores to stop or at least to mute such activities. Have respect for the starving Jews staring through the windows, waiting for handouts, pleading for the right to the garbage cans. Please, have pity for the children running to lap up the spilled soup or slops from the ground, like dogs, unmindful of kicks and curses.

The pleas go unheeded.

There is a cafe at 2 Leszno Street that presents a nightly floor show, and another at Tlomackie. Both are owned by renegade Jews in collusion with members of the Gestapo.

The worst of all is the Britannia. It caters to Jewish Gestapo agents, Jewish police, high-ranking smugglers, rich merchants trading with money-loving

Germans, prostitutes, pushers, the Leszno Street Thirteen, informers, all degrees of collaborators. The feasting, dancing, jazz bands, sex continue from dusk to dawn. At the entrance a constantly changing contingent of beggers to plead for crumbs, for coins. Each night, at the curbs, their bodies replace the bodies of the beggars who had crowded the entrance the night before.

As promised, I treat my gang to an evening at the Britannia.

Arriving home at dawn after having exchanged farewells with One-Eye and Greasehead and the others, I find my father gone and everyone else in the apartment in panic. My mother hides in a corner, eyes wide but seeing nothing. She rocks back and forth. I take her in my arms and talk to her, but she does not respond. Others tell me what happened.

The Germans broke into the apartment last night, looking for me. They took my father hostage: if Gideon does not turn himself in within twenty-four hours, the Germans will kill his father.

I hear the words. And other words.

My mother raced after them in the streets. My father shouted to her to go back. She refused. He called, in Yiddish, for her to tell me to hold out, to never surrender, to survive. The Germans beat him to the ground with their rifle butts. My father leaped to his feet and grabbed the SS officer in charge, hugged him, continued hugging him until the grenade in my Father's pocket, the grenade he must have primed, exploded, killing the German and himself.

Rocking my mother in my arms, I assure her that I will not leave the ghetto again. Several in the room, behind my mother's back, shake their fists at me. Too late, my Aunt Pola says before her husband can silence her, too late for such fine sentiments.

8

There will be no journey through Warsaw to visit Grandmother and Sonia. Mother, held in my arms, sees nothing. My Aunt Pola takes Mother from me and leads her to the room that is used as a toilet.

I lie beside my mother all night, trying to warm her shivering body with my own. As a little boy I would run to my parents' room and crawl into bed and slide under the eiderdown comforter, squeezing between their bodies, loving their warmth. There is no warmth now.

Dr. Korczak sends a messenger the next day. Not to complain about Mother's absence or to ask if and when she plans to return to the orphanage, but to ask if she is well, if there is anything he can do.

I remain in the apartment during the three days of my mother's near coma. One-Eye does not appear, but one of the Jewish porters brings a message relayed through several intermediaries. "Where are you? When do we work? Answer." I try to reply but cannot seem to be able to make a decision. Nothing seems important at the moment except to somehow demonstrate to my mother my love and my regret. Regret not just for my father's death, but for his dying without our reconciliation. I know that everyone is waiting: One-Eye, the gang, the ghetto porters, the various liaisons already established within the network of the operation Yankele had organized. But they are no longer important, any of them.

Late in the afternoon of the third day, Mother rises. She is very thin, and the bones of her face almost protrude through the gray skin. She sits with me the way she once did, just the two of us, talking. We say nothing about Father, about the war, about the ghetto. We talk of ourselves, how each of us feels about being a Jew.

In the strangely easy, natural conversation, neither of us sounds religious, pretentiously philosophical. We might be talking about how we feel about a play we've just attended, or a movie, or a gathering at a friend's home. She talks about an event several years before, when she threatened to organize the women in a rebellion against segregation in the synagogue, with men on the ground floor and women in the balcony. She laughs. How important that seemed then, she says, how trivial now.

She talks about my being out of their protection, out of reach of their attention. She asks questions about my activities, without being critical or punitive. What have I done with all the money I've earned? My contributions to the organizations, to the hospitals, to the orphanages, to the dying Jews in the streets, will, I feel, appear to be bribes to buy her respect, her admiration. My silence brings a mild, almost chiding rebuke.

A good Jew would have shared, would have cared about other Jews who need care. She is simply defining what she and my father have always considered to be *a good Jew.* Good, she says, is God with an extra *o.* "There is something special in being a Jew. Look at us, Gideon. We are Poles, aren't we? But when we talk of other Poles who are Gentiles, we call them Poles; and when we talk of ourselves, who are also Polish, we call ourselves Jews. We are Jews first and then Poles. It is the same all over Europe.

We are tied together not by being German or French or Polish, but by being Jews. Jews can decide if they want to remain Germans or French or Poles, but they *are* Jews. No decision is necessary. Or possible."

I complain that I should have studied the Torah harder, and Jewish history, and my mother confides to me she now shares my father's regrets that involvements in their own ghetto work had interrupted plans for me to complete my bar mitzvah.

This is the first reference to what is suggested, by the tone of my mother's voice as well as the quivering clasp of her hands, to have been a major neglect. I want to say it is not important, but I think of how, several times, I had been on the verge of mentioning it to Yankele. It had obviously been a disappointment, that ignored initiation into manhood. I had been wounded by my mother and father choosing to become involved in something more important to them than that eternal ritual of confirmation. Had I mentioned it to Yankele, there would have been jokes and teasing. *Ah, little Gideon,* he would have said, *no ritual can make you a man. You make yourself a man.* I can almost hear him speaking. But it is my mother's voice.

She kisses me. "You don't have to study Judaism to be a Jew. You simply are. You have no choice.

You can deny it but that's like denying your eyes are blue. I do not worry about you now, Gideon. For a while, yes, I worried. No more. You will survive; you will always be a Jew. Twenty, thirty years from now, when you are married and have children of your own, think back on our talk today. Even that far away from today, you will be a strong Jew. I promise."

She rises. She must go to the orphanage. There is work to do. The children are frightened. Unlike me, they have no mother to reassure them during these terrible days.

She pats my cheek, kisses both of my eyes, and says I have proven myself capable of surviving. My father had known that they, he and she, had, if nothing else, prepared me well for survival by what they did right as well as what they did wrong. She holds my face, studies me lovingly, kisses me once more, and then, while holding the door open, she says, with a revived spark of that old, almost arrogant toughness in her pose, that I should remember the children.

She throws me a kiss and leaves.

I stay in the apartment all day. I am not interested in eating, even if food were available. I sit silent, motionless, in the same chair in which my mother had sat. Others who live in the rooms come and go, talk to me, but I do not respond. I think of my father. I see him priming the grenade in his pocket; I see him leaping to grab and hug the German, trapping him in his fatal embrace; I hear the explosion. If the Germans could capture my father, they must be the supermen they claim to be. Are they the master race? Are Jews inferior? Weak? Ineffectual? How else explain the ghetto?

A hint of vengeance stirs. I will not be weak; I will not be ineffectual. An eye for an eye, a tooth . . . But will a dead German or ten dead Germans bring my father back to life?

A visitor from Aryan Warsaw. One-Eye.

Where have I been? Did I get the messages? Why didn't I respond? Plans have been made, bribes have been paid.

My uneasy relatives shrink against the wall, fearful that this Polish thug can only mean betrayal and death. I tell One-Eye what has happened. He shrugs, looks about him at the crowded, foul-smelling room, at the emaciated and ragged Jews. Do I want to leave this place? Come live with him? Maybe we'll join the PPR, the partisans. He grins. I'd look fine in a uniform.

The people in the apartment don't know what to do about this. Here is a Polish thug, the worst kind of anti-Semite, here he is in the ghetto wearing a Star of David on his arm, giving little Gideon pep talks.

The visit does give me strength. I promise to meet him in three or four days at the cafe where we'd first made our pact to support each other, to work together. He adjusts his armband and departs.

I awaken at dawn to the sound of powerful motors.

From the window where all my relatives are kneeling and weeping, I see, down in the street, ten or twelve big army trucks. The predicted *Aktion* is under way.

Soldiers are pulling men, women, children out of buildings and throwing them into trucks. Women are screaming for their babies who have been tossed into other trucks. Fathers struggle to remain with their families. The soldiers—Germans mixed with Lithuanians and Ukrainians—are using their rifle butts freely. I hear boots on the stairs. The people inside the apartment have gathered in the center of the room. They've eluded the Germans until today, but now there is no more escape.

While rifle butts slam at the locked door, I rush up into the attic and out through a skylight and onto the roof.

My earlier homework is about to pay off. I've learned my lessons well.

The zinc roof is hot. I lie on my back beside a chimney as the noise below grows louder. Screams and shots intermingle. Such a clear blue sky, I think, to have to gaze down on such human misery.

I ease up toward the ridge, taking care to keep my head and body pressed tightly against the metal. When I glance down, I see Dr. Korczak, wearing a neat blue suit, a white shirt, a dark tie. His shoes are polished. There is a line of children, all of whom have been scrubbed and dressed in clean clothes, as if ready for an outing in the park. They are in pairs and holding hands.

Dr. Korczak, a child on either side, takes their hands. Several women, also neatly dressed, move among the children who follow, patting their heads, squeezing their shoulders, adjusting a collar here, a shoelace there. At the end of the line, hair combed, face powdered, smiling, directing the children in a song, is my mother. She is youthful again. She strides forward, tall and straight, free, independent, almost swaggering. It is the mother of my young boyhood before the war.

As the column of children moves toward the trucks (and, I know now, toward freight cars waiting two miles away), my mother does not look back. I hear her strong voice above all the others. Pure, clear, like a fine thin bell. I never see her again.

Evening. It is warm but I am shivering. I am still on the roof.

I cross to Nalewki Street, to Gesia, to Zamenhofa, to Mila. The roofs are my allies; more than my allies, they are my friends. I start across a narrow catwalk between two roofs, intending to reach Kupiecka Street. I am halfway across when a door opens and a Ukrainian soldier appears. He aims his rifle at me. "Wait," I call in Polish. "I have a beautiful woman."

I'm not sure he understands what I have said, so I try again, letting my hands shape the word in the air. I see his trigger finger relaxing. He grins and a gold front tooth gleams. "Gold," I say. "Much gold."

He nods and his grin widens. "Go," he says. "I go after." His Polish is good enough to convince me that he has understood mine.

As I move along the catwalk I have to remind myself to remain calm, to exploit everything I've learned in my various escapes from Germans and Blues and Jewish police. I feign great fear, I cringe in servility. I slump my shoulders, wring my hands, and try unsuccessfully to cry. "Don't shoot me. Please. Much gold. Very beautiful woman."

The Ukrainian backs up until he is against the door and he dips the rifle, ordering me forward. As I push past him, the front rifle sight is less than an inch from my head. To appear even smaller than I am, I hunch my shoulders and bend my knees. My performance seems to convince him.

Taking advantage of the brief moment of his arrogant self-assurance, I straighten my knees and spring. My head butts him in the groin. My hands, thrown upward, knock the rifle from his fingers as a bullet whistles past my cheek. The explosion deafens me and I hear nothing as the body, like a stunt actor in a silent movie, slides down and over the edge of the roof. The rifle is in my hands.

9

For months after my mother strides out of my life, I live like a robot. The *Aktion* of early August has accomplished much of its purpose. The survivors in the ghetto are stunned, depressed almost to total apathy. Without knowing why, or caring, I go on living. But now the bond, the working agreement, with One-Eye's gang is changed. Most of Yankele's porters are no longer alive. And I am less interested in food, more interested in the ghetto's arsenal.

Whatever I must do to get money to buy weapons, I do. Money not only supports my now sporadic relationship with One-Eye and the others, it continues what my father had begun. He and others were dedicated to building up a resistance army. Though late, I join their mission.

The summer passes. And the cold wet autumn, during which I am nearly captured, nearly shot every day. Nearly. My luck continues. And my agility. Cornered, rounded up, thrown into trucks, I need only the blink of a guard's eye, the turn of his head, to leap free, to dash into streets or alleys, to disappear into crowds.

Survive, Gideon. My father's voice rides the blood through my heart. *At any cost . . .*

As I roam the ghetto, I see the results of the work accomplished by my father and the others who had been struggling to rouse the Jews to defend themselves.

People who once believed the presence of the Germans to be temporary and their intentions to annihilate every Jew in Europe exaggerated, misunderstood, are now convinced.

There is not a house or an apartment or a shop or a factory that does not have its secret rooms, chambers within chambers, tunnels leading not just from room to room but from building to building, street to street. Strategic rooms and buildings have been rebuilt to serve as fortifications or bunkers when such service will be necessary. It is no longer a matter now of if, but when.

Hundreds of thousands of Jews of all ages have been shot or beaten to death in the streets and their homes, worked or gassed to death in Sobibor, Auschwitz, Treblinka.

What had once been more than a half-million Jews in this ghetto are now, in January, 1943, reduced to little more than fifty thousand. Almost all are resigned to their death. ZOB, the Jewish Fighting Organization, consists of men and women and children with many different hopes and fears and philosophies, but now with one motive: to make the German SS and Gestapo pay dearly for every Jewish life taken in the past and every Jewish life to be taken in the future.

And so weapons become a mass preoccupation. In the entire ghetto there can't be more than thirty or forty machine guns, no more than a hundred rifles, a hundred handguns, perhaps a hundred pounds of explosives. There are hidden stocks of grenades and material for our homemade bombs but not a single artillery piece. A puny arsenal to face the most formidable fighting force ever created by man. But we have no choice.

The promises from our so-called Allies will not be kept. We know that now. How we long to see British bombers in the sky above Warsaw, parachutes carrying weapons and ammunition to our fighting forces. Once we prayed every hour of every day for a single word of encouragement from our idol, Franklin Delano Roosevelt. His silence matches Stalin's. The most cynical voices insist that they—Roosevelt and Stalin and Churchill—hope for success for the German's extermination plan.

On the Aryan side of the wall, on Gornoslaska Street, a center for the collection of arms is set up at the home of a Polish Gentile worker. He helps the Jews buy and smuggle arms. I begin again the money-making procedures I'd learned so well from Yankele. I call in One-Eye and the gang. Money for arms.

A Polish National Army captain, Henry Iwanski, struggles against tradition and compatriots and the demands of his own underground forces, and detours weapons to the ghetto army. Why? (Many years later, after at least five members of his own family had been massacred by the Germans, Captain—then Major—Iwanski was asked why he risked his life to help the Jews. "When the Jew cries, I cry," he said.

"When a Jew suffers, I am a Jew. All are of my nation, for I am a man." This from a man who had been wounded in a lung, leg, and arm; who was wounded twice more in the Warsaw uprising of August, 1944; who, after the war, was arrested by the Polish Communist government for fighting not for the workers but only for the intellectuals and the rich; who was then imprisoned for seven years; who, today, impoverished and ill, remains in Warsaw, nursing his wife, Wictoria, who, while nursing a sick Jewish girl, caught the tuberculosis from which she still suffers.)

The process of preparation is dangerous and time-consuming. Meetings to discuss military strategy, smuggling, construction of tunnels, preparation of hiding places and bunkers, stockpiling of food and fighting supplies—all must be done without attracting the attention not only of the Germans and Ukrainians and dangerous Poles, but also of near-demented Jews who, hoping to save their lives, would carry information to the enemy.

There is a great market at Kazimierz Square where anything can be purchased. Even weapons. Guards at ammunition dumps steal guns and ammunition

101

and arrange deliveries to our representatives. German soldiers, renegades and runaways, sell us weapons, usually but not always through our intermediaries. Poles who work in arms factories bring out weapons in pieces, assemble them at home, and sell them to us.

For a brief period in January, German attention is diverted from the ghetto. German units, needing slave labor, attack Polish towns and villages, dragging Gentile men, women, and children to labor camps.

So the Polish Gentiles have a taste of what Polish Jews—and Jews from every country Germany has overrun—have been enduring for years. Considering the Poles akin to animals, the Germans treat the country like one large hunting preserve. Humans are legitimate quarry.

At six o'clock in the morning of January 18, the ghetto streets that house the slave laborers for nearby German shops and factories are filled with shouts of German soldiers, the blast of truck horns, the rumble of motors, the rapid-firing German machine guns. The Germans and their hired killers, the Ukrainians and the Lithuanians, pull people into the streets and march them toward the collecting station, the *Umschlagplatz,* from where, for the last six months, thousands of trains have hauled almost a half-million Jews to the gas chambers of Treblinka. Jewish workers on their way to German factories are herded into the lines. Work cards, documents once as precious as jewels, are worthless. It is the beginning of the Germans' final push, the final *Aktion,* to clear out the ghetto, to complete the annihilation of the Warsaw Jews.

The Germans have gone into action so quickly, so efficiently, that the Jewish Fighting Organization, ZOB, is taken by surprise. There is little time to rush to battle sites, to put prearranged tactical plans into operation.

Four groups do manage to function: the Zamenhofa, the Mila, the Muranowska, and the Franciszkanska. At those four streets, our fighters open fire with rifles and grenades.

More than twenty Germans and Ukrainians are killed. Many more are wounded.

For the first time, Jews hear Germans screaming in pain. Jews have killed Germans. Jewish soldiers are fighting back.

The Ukrainians and Lithuanians break and run. The Germans follow.

Jewish fighters in the ghetto of Warsaw have put the mighty German army in retreat.

Inside and outside the ghetto the stories of the appearance of a Jewish fighting unit electrify the people. The will of every Jew to fight back is kindled, flames brighter. The Polish underground press enthusiastically welcomes the battle of January 18. From the official underground Polish army, Armia Krajowa, we receive pistols and ammunition. Allies on the Aryan side of the ghetto, Jew and Gentile, escort shipments of arms into the ghetto.

In the ghetto streets, German soldiers no longer walk alone.

A delicate but essential part of our battle plan must be accomplished immediately. Volunteers are requested to track down every Jewish Gestapo agent in the ghetto and kill them. Having learned that Jewish Gestapo agents had been responsible for my father's death, I volunteer. Because of my experience and my reputation, I am placed in charge of a group of four, all of whom are older than I.

Jew killing Jew. None of us finds it easy. But security is more important now than sentiment.

The mission is accomplished in two days and one night.

The morale of every fighting group is strengthened, their sense of themselves as Jews, as Jewish fighters, heightened. I wonder about Yankele. Where would he be, what would he be doing, what would he be feeling?

Adult members of the ghetto are taxed for money to buy arms. Those wealthy Jews who refuse to pay are arrested. Very few Jews now argue that hostility toward the Germans will only anger them and make them more vicious.

I wish my father were alive. He would see those early warnings of his taken up by hundreds of voices now, shouted from fighter to fighter. If he could only see the slogans painted on the walls, printed on posters: REFUSE TO GO WILLINGLY TO THE SLAUGHTER! FIGHT BACK!!

During the next three weeks, whenever the Germans try to revive their kidnappings and evacuations, workers set fire to factory supplies, to the shops, to the warehouses. Wagons loaded with stockpiled leather and textiles are set ablaze. The Germans will have to find their uniforms and holsters and boots elsewhere. At the *Umschlagplatz,* a group of workers on their way to Treblinka refuses to enter the freight cars. One youth, a former labor organizer, urges the crowd not to go willingly. Everyone must fight, must resist. The guards open fire, killing him and a hundred other protesters.

We wait inside the ghetto and prepare, selecting defensive positions. A few Jews, continuing successful passage in and out of the ghetto, bring, along with an occasional weapon, something almost as important: information.

In late January we hear that Jews are being transported from the Theresienstadt ghetto to Auschwitz.

February 2 we hear that the entire German Sixth Army has surrendered at Stalingrad. Oh, how we cheer at this, thinking that concessions must surely follow. Nothing changes. In fact, three weeks later we receive news that Jewish armament workers in Berlin have been deported to Auschwitz.

On March 13 there are two announcements that thrill and chill the ghetto. First: officers of Germany's Central Army Group in the Soviet Union have tried to assassinate Hitler. They failed. Second: new crematoriums have opened at Auschwitz.

In late March or early April, someone smuggles a newspaper into the ghetto. It is so tattered it is barely legible, but there is no doubt about the content of the major story. There is to be an international conference in Bermuda, establishing quotas for refugees from Occupied France. Quotas. Jews, a certain number of you might live. *We* will decide, Jews.

Special battle units of ZOB are now placed in strategically located houses. I am in charge of one of the units.

In my unit are eight men and two women. I refer to them as men and women, though several are as young as I. If they are to die, what better time and place than now? Their parents kiss them farewell.

In what every Jew knows might well be the final hour of the ghetto, we prepare ourselves. We are determined that before we die, we will taste at least a small bit of revenge.

The three-year nightmare, I think, is about to end. I do not know that another is about to begin.

April 18. Sunday. At night our scouts listen for the faintest sound of motors or boots that might indicate movement of German troops or equipment. Near midnight, Polish police begin to surround the ghetto. Fighters are assigned to their posts and we distribute weapons and ammunition. And supplies of potassium cyanide, so we can kill ourselves if about to be captured.

By 2:00 A.M., Ukrainian, Latvian, and SS units are outside the ghetto walls.

April 19. Monday. Infantry and armored units of the German army that has devastated three-fourths of the continent begin their attack on the Warsaw ghetto. That day is the first day of the festival of Passover.

Why is this night different from all other nights?

The question, asked the first night of every Passover down through thousands of years, is about to be answered. The Germans are about to hear the answer loud and clear.

Poland capitulated in twenty-six days. Holland capitulated in five days. Belgium capitulated in eighteen days. Luxembourg capitulated in one day. Yugoslavia capitulated in eleven days. Greece capitulated in fourteen days. The tiny starving army of untrained Jews with almost no military equipment denied victory to the mighty German army for one full month.

10

The sun is bright. A warm spring day.

Black-uniformed battalions of death, they march into the ghetto in full battle dress. With armored carriers, tanks, machine guns. Down Zamenhofa they come, the infantry striding as if on parade. They approach Franciszkanska, Mila, Muranowska.

The signal has gone out through the ghetto. We wait at our assigned battle stations. How insignificant, comic, we would appear, if we were seen. But the Germans see only empty streets, silent buildings.

The Germans and their Slav allies advance, certain that their mere appearance must have the Jewish bandits, as we are called, shivering in our ragged clothes.

The troops reach Mila Street. From opposite corners—from 29 Zamenhofa and 38 Zamenhofa—there is a sudden shower of flaming gasoline-filled bottles and grenades. Many Germans fall dead. The black-clad supermen are crawling and flopping about in the street. Two tanks erupt in flames, their crews perishing without a chance to escape. A tiny, as yet insignificant, payment for the millions of Jews already and yet to be incinerated.

Again the mighty warriors of the eternal Third Reich retreat before the onslaught of the Jew warriors.

Almost before the German bodies left behind have stopped breathing, our fighters are upon them, stripping them of their helmets, of uniforms, of boots, especially of their precious weapons and grenades and ammunition.

Several are still alive. They remain alive only a moment. Rivka, one of the women in my unit, has had three baby brothers and both of her parents gassed at Treblinka. Rivka examines each body. When she finds one alive she shoots him.

We return to our bunker, regroup, settle down and wait for the inevitable counterattack.

110

Within the hour the ghetto's electricity and water are turned off. The canteens removed from the German bodies—which lie stiff in the spring sunshine—prove useful.

They return later in the morning.

They know they are in combat and not just on field maneuvers. General Stroop, the SS commander of the Warsaw ghetto, knows now that the ghetto will have to be taken house by house.

Singly, in small groups, the German soldiers cover each other's advance, spraying roofs and windows and doorways with machinegun fire. They run hunched over, against the walls; they no longer stride down the middle of the street.

No opposition appears. Do they think that the Jews have used the last of their ammunition, the last of their will to fight? Had the previous resistance been the action of a few fools? They are soon informed of the true situation. Another shower of gasoline-filled bottles and grenades and dynamite bombs from windows and roofs and attics creates havoc once again among the black-uniformed troops. A three-hundred man unit of elite SS troops that has penetrated past Walowa Street is almost completely destroyed by an electrically ignited mine planted by our fighters at 3032 Swietorjerska.

As more German units are thrown into the battle—not just platoons but entire companies—our fighters withdraw through attics, across the roofs, through the tunnels.

More German units arrive, but they have to battle for every foot of every street, every floor of every building. The streets are filled with German bodies. Burning tanks and armored cars block the streets, so the German ambulances cannot get through to rescue their wounded. As each building is given up and our fighters retreat, the Germans set fire to every building they capture.

The German advance is guaranteed, but it is also costly. Too costly. They withdraw again. We return to those buildings near the flames. Word of our victory has reached the rear. There are cries of elation, prayers of thanksgiving. Our elation and our prayers are cut short. The Germans, using flamethrowers, set fire to entire blocks of buildings. While they wait for us to be incinerated, their artillery pieces, located outside the ghetto, out of the range of our small arms and our homemade explosives and grenades, lob shell after shell into the burning ghetto.

At one point my unit—seven of us now, and none of us over seventeen—is trapped. Flames surround us. It seems that earth and sky are on fire. The asphalt streets are rivers of melted tar; cobblestones are steaming. Rags protect the feet. Houses collapse, sending up explosions of sparks and flames. Many Jews choose to remain within the flames, to burn to death rather than let themselves be captured and hauled to Treblinka.

We wrap our feet in rags and break through a burning wall and race along the streets and into a house not yet aflame.

The air is thick and sweet with the stench of burning bodies.

Along every street, people are jumping from fourth and fifth floors of smoke- and flame-covered buildings. Mothers hurl babies from rooftops to spare them the agony of burning to death, and then the mothers leap after them.

The Germans are trying desperately to end it. More and more troop carriers and tanks are brought up, pushing the flaming obstacles out of the way, to clear a path. But they in turn catch fire.

There is no rear area now. Everyone is fighting. Women, men, children. Those who have no weapons act as couriers, as medics, as waterbearers when they can find water. A woman in a wheelchair seems to have a charmed life as she rolls about in the street,

113

collecting German canteens. The entire German army seems to be firing at her, but she remains unscathed, wheeling herself into the lobby of a building with ten or fifteen canteens in her lap.

Using SS and regular infantry uniforms we collected from earlier attacks, our fighters pose as Germans, move close enough to tanks, personnel carriers, and individual soldiers to use our rifles and revolvers. We concentrate on officers. I swagger through the smoke in my SS uniform, which obviously has not been tailored to my body. I carry myself with the disdain I know the former owner would feel for the fifteen-year-old Jew now wearing it. I recognize an *Obersturmfuhrer* who had shot at bodies falling from the rooftops. From behind a tank, using a rifle taken from a dead German, I fire twice at the nose above the mustache, and then I fall back into the rolling clouds of black smoke.

After a week of battle, it is known that the German press has been reporting the ghetto resistance as the refusal of Jews to work. The illegal Polish press has been covering our battle sympathetically, comparing our heroism to that of Bar Kokba and his troops, who rebelled against the Roman armies. Daily communiques describe the bitter Jewish resistance to the

Third Reich's army, identifying the name and character of specific German units, the deadly results of their artillery, the number of German soldiers killed and wounded.

Unfortunately, the average Pole is not always sympathetic. Jews hiding in Aryan Warsaw find ways to return to the ghetto so they might fight and, if necessary, die with their people. They tell of crowds of Poles observing the battle from Swietojerska Street and Krasinsky Square. Many react favorably to the destruction of the Jews, assuring their children or their companions that as soon as the Jews are destroyed the Germans will leave Poland.

The few Jewish agents still operating in Aryan Warsaw fail to arouse the organized Polish underground to give us actual physical support. The Poles argue that an open fight at this time would mean their own extermination. We request that they demonstrate their support by filling the streets with their protestors. The underground refuses to organize street demonstrations.

In the early part of the uprising, the Jewish underground in Aryan Warsaw issues a message to the Polish people. Through our inefficient communication system (messages are delivered to the Polish underground radio station, and from there to the Polish government-in-exile in London, and from there through BBC, radio station Swit, and others), the news is broadcast back to Poland and the rest of the world.

Here—my memory refreshed by Bernard Goldstein's *The Stars Bear Witness*—is that message.

> Poles, citizens, soldiers of freedom. Through the thunder of artillery which is shelling our homes, our mothers, wives, and children; through the sound of machine-guns; through clouds of smoke and fire; over the streams of blood which flow in the murdered ghetto of Warsaw; we, the prisoners of the ghetto, send you our heartfelt brotherly greeting.
>
> We know that you watch with heartbreak, with tears of sympathy, with horror and amazement, for the outcome of the struggle we have been carrying on for several days with the hateful occupier.
>
> Be assured that every threshold in the ghetto will remain, as it has been until now, a fortress; that though we may all perish in this struggle, we will not surrender; that we breathe as you do with a thirst for vengeance and punishment for the crimes of our common enemy.
>
> This is a fight for your freedom and ours, for your and our human, social, and national pride! We will

avenge the crimes of Auschwitz, Treblinka, Belzec, and Maidanek! Long live the brotherhood of blood and arms of Fighting Poland! Long live Freedom! Death to the executioners! A fight unto death with the occupier!

Jewish Fighting Organizations
April 23, 1943

And the ghetto burns.

As the flames consume more and more streets in the Warsaw ghetto, the mighty Allied armies are in action against the Germans. Great military struggles are taking place in Europe, in the air and on the seas.

Appeals from the Warsaw ghetto are answered with silence.

Through our contact with the underground in Aryan Warsaw, we receive the news that Artur Ziygelbojm, the Jewish representative to the Polish National Council in London, protests the silence. How can the world ignore the torture and killing of millions of his brothers and sisters?

We receive a copy of the letter he writes to the callous world.

I cannot be silent—I cannot live—while remnants of the Jewish people of Poland, of whom I am a representative, are perishing. My comrades in the Warsaw ghetto took weapons in their hands on that last heroic impulse. It was not my destiny to die there with them, but I belong to them, and in their mass graves.

By my death I wish to express my strongest protest against the inactivity with which the world is looking on and permitting the extermination of my people.

I know how little human life is worth today, but as I was unable to do anything during my life, perhaps by my death I shall contribute to breaking down the indifference of those who may now—at the last moment—rescue the few Polish Jews still alive from certain annihilation. My life belongs to the Jewish people of Poland and I therefore give it to them. I wish that this remaining handful of the original several millions of Polish Jews could live to see the liberation of a new world of freedom, and the justice of true Socialism. I believe that such a Poland will arise and that such a world will come.

The letter, if published at all, is lost among the news items about the war.

The suicide of Ziygelbojm assures us in the ghetto that there is no hope.

11

Fire and black smoke spill out of the ghetto. Remnants of Jewish units hold out in cellars, in concealed bunkers. The Germans introduce a new weapon. Gas. It is shot into hiding places or dropped in cannisters.

Of my original unit of ten members, only three remain: two others and I. One of the other two is Rivka. Tall, lean, unwashed, covered with ash and dust, her hair singed by flames, she looks like an African. Exhausted, she drags one foot after the other.

It is the twenty-fourth day of the German attack. What organizational control existed among the Jews at the beginning has deteriorated to scattered individuals and units communicating with each other by courier when possible. More often, we all remain ignorant of what streets have been taken, what buildings will offer protection, who is dead, who remains alive.

Some are determined never to surrender to the Germans. They kill themselves. Some argue that suicide is contrary to our purpose. Why kill yourself when you can perhaps kill a German during the battle in which you will be killed? In some cases the seriously wounded cannot be saved or moved, and beg us to kill them. We do. Other times we carry the less seriously wounded with us, always hoping that a miracle of Russian or American or British intervention will save us all.

The Germans have destroyed almost all of what had been the ghetto. But resistance continues: single snipers acting alone, or suicide units determined to make the Germans pay dearly for their efforts.

I have no doubts about my intentions. I intend to survive; I am determined to survive. No suicide for me. I will escape the ghetto.

I have heard of others who have already escaped through the sewers. I know a group is forming now to try another escape. The streets and walls are under such thorough German control that the sewers are our final hope.

Rivka and the other survivor in my unit, a lanky, bearded former rabbinical student named Abraham, hear my plan. We have three revolvers and two rifles and twelve grenades. We have about ten rounds left for each weapon. With three bullets to be kept for ourselves and with probably half of our fired rounds missing their targets, we could kill as many as ten or twelve Germans. Before we kill ourselves. (Their words. Not mine. *Gideon, you will survive.* Those are my words.) Is it worth the effort? If we all try to escape through the sewers and even one of us makes it, we can still be sure more than four Germans will be killed.

The three of us agree. We will join the others who are planning an escape through the sewers. Rivka pleads patience. As a courier between our forces and the Polish underground, she has moved in and out of the ghetto more, perhaps, than any other Jew. She still has contacts, she says: she has secret doors. Give her time. For groups of us to escape, we must use the sewers. She has a friend in the Polish underground in the Aryan section and will appeal to him for help.

A complex web of tunnels and aqueducts, the underground sewer system carries the filth of the entire city of Warsaw. Others who have preceded us, ignorant of the design of the system, have either not made it up through the exits or have drowned or suffocated en route. Rivka tells us her friend has friends who can get us maps of the sewer system.

Neither Abraham nor I have much hope, but we agree to let her try. Rivka sleeps for a few hours before she leaves. As we embrace and bid her farewell, we review our plans. We will meet the next day at a demolished house on Mila or, the day after that, in the charred cellar of a piece of house on Zamenhofa.

She departs in good cheer, as if she has no doubt whatever that we will be seeing each other again.

During what remains of the evening, Abraham and I hide in the cellar of a building already burned to the ground and passed hourly by columns of German soldiers going into the ghetto to kill more Jews and burn more buildings. There are three corpses in the cellar, already half-eaten by the cat-sized rats. We try to frighten the rats away, but we dare not make noise. The rats, squatting on tops of the corpses, tearing out chunks of flesh, consider us with their beady eyes but refuse to be intimidated. I close my eyes. I cannot see them, but I can hear them chewing.

Am I at the end of my fifteen years of charmed life? I have evaded the Germans and the Ukrainians and the Lithuanians and the Polish Blues and the Jewish police. I have been a thief and a smuggler and a killer. My mother and father are dead, as are most of my relatives and friends. Why have I survived this long? I think of Sonia and Grandmother. Have they managed to survive? Will I ever know? If Sonia does live and grows to be a woman, a mother, what will she remember of her own mother? Of her father? Of me, her brother?

I—her brother, who once carried her on his shoulders through the park—am probably already forgotten.

At twenty minutes past noon the next day, Abraham and I leave our refuge. For almost two hours we crawl through the smoking rubble to Mila Street. Rivka is there, waiting for us. With her are two young Poles. They once worked in the city's sewer system and are now fighting in the Polish underground army. They have maps of the entire system. It is obvious from their appearance and their stench that they have returned here by way of the sewers. Movement aboveground, Rivka tells us, is impossible. She would not try it again. They had reentered the ghetto through the sewer opening on Mila, near Smocza. We will all leave through the same opening.

The Germans surround 18 Mila, the headquarters of ZOB, the Jewish Fighting Organization. They try for two hours to storm the bunker, but are thrown back each time. They rely on poison gas, and succeed.

May 14. Now. No more waiting. May 14 is Sonia's birthday. I want to escape now.

Thirty of us, including Rivka and Abraham and the two Poles, make our way through the sewers toward Prosta Street. There are booby-trapped barbed-wire cages that bar the various passages, but we cut our way through them.

We wade, swim, help each other through the stench and muck. Rivka shakes her head. She can go no farther, she says. Leave her. The others of us should go on. I hold her up. Another man, one of the Poles, helps me, and together we manage to keep her head above the slime.

For twenty-four hours we make our way through the sewers, lumps of garbage and human waste floating past our chins, dead bodies of former comrades prodding us, their bloated faces reminding us to keep them in our memories. Our original thirty is reduced to nineteen. Nineteen not including Abraham. The missing have slid beneath the surface, some protesting, striking out feebly, others without a sound. One of those had been Abraham.

It is night when we reach the Prosta Street sewer exit. The two trucks that are supposed to pick us up have not arrived. Or have they arrived and been captured? We are at our destination, but we dare not climb to the street because we would be without transportation.

We wait. Three hours, four. Five.

There is a groan, a sigh, as someone slides under the sewage.

Rivka clings to us, the Pole and me, pleading for water. Desperate with thirst, she tries to drink the muck at her chin, but we do not let her. I hold her head up by pulling at her hair, keeping her mouth above the surface. A while longer, I say. A few minutes more.

Six hours. Seven.

Above us it is early morning. The streets will be filled with crowds.

The word comes. The trucks have arrived. There is a surge toward the exit. I lose my grip on Rivka. She slides through my hands. I push at the bodies around me, dive beneath the slime. The Pole, her special friend, dives with me. We feel for her with our hands and feet. Five minutes, ten, fifteen, we dive and surface and dive.

The trucks are almost loaded. Two or three more people climb the ladder. The driver shouts down at us. He cannot wait. All the other lives are being risked by our delay. I climb the ladder, the sewage so heavy on my body I can barely drag myself through the opening. Farewell, my beloved Rivka. And farewell, her loyal Polish friend.

Ours is the last group to escape through the sewers. The Germans fill every branch of the system beneath the ghetto with poison gas.

Of the thirty who began the escape attempt, fourteen have succeeded.

General Stroop orders the great synagogue destroyed. The ultimate symbol of Judaism.

126

At 8:15 the morning of May 16, a German sapper officer passes the electric detonator to General Jürgen Stroop, SS commander of the Warsaw ghetto operation. Shouting "Heil Hitler!" he presses the button.

That evening General Stroop sends a cable to General Krüger in Krakow. "The famous Jewish quarter of Warsaw no longer exists."

Stroop reports to Berlin that exactly 56,065 Jews have been captured or killed since the *Grosse Aktion* against the Warsaw ghetto started. Thousands more are buried in the rubble, beyond statistical verification.

We who escaped continue to hear occasional bursts of machine-gun fire from the rubble of the ghetto for weeks after May 16.

We hide in Lomiank Forest while the search goes on for the people who will dare to house the ghetto survivors. Informers are everywhere. How long can we hide here before we are betrayed to the Germans?

Poles who are known to have been friendly are now frightened by the increased attention of the Germans to non-Jews. Nazis have been attacking all Poles: Catholic and Protestant, old and young, men and women and children.

The Gestapo is everywhere. Along with a new hazard. *Schmaltzovniks.* Gangs of thugs who prey on Jews, demanding their fat, meaning their money. The Yiddish term for fat is *schmaltz.* So the term *schmaltzovniks.* They are beating up Jews, taking their money, and then handing them over to the Gestapo for extra bonuses.

We appeal to the Polish underground to destroy these thugs, but the underground refuses to act.

We continue to receive messages through Polish workers recruited by the Germans to clean up the ruins. There are still Jews in the bunkers, fighting, begging for food.

Six of us make a weak effort to return with food and water. Of the six in the unit, two of us succeed. A man who was once a champion swimmer, and I. The swimming champion loses both legs when a grenade explodes in our last effort to breach the wall. He begs me to shoot him. I don't have to. He dies almost immediately in my arms.

The Germans build two lines of railroad tracks to carry their loot from the ghetto. The laborers who build the tracks are Poles. There are no more Jews left to work.

It is June. I will die if I remain one more day in the cellar where I have hidden, from which I have made nightly forays for food. Not one more day. I think constantly, sometimes perhaps in delirium, of Sonia. She must have survived. I have to know. Someone must be left. I am endangering her life as well as my own by leaving the cellar, but I no longer care. I must touch Sonia.

In the street, moving from doorway to doorway, shadow to shadow, I listen for sounds of resistance from the ghetto. Not a sound.

I am jumped by three *schmaltzovniks*. I fight back, losing my knife in the side of one of them. I am knocked unconscious. I wake up in a boxcar, held upright by the bodies crushed against me. Prayers, sobs, screams drown out the sounds of the wheels. I am on the way to Treblinka.

12

A small railway station. "Picturesque," a tourist brochure might have advised some years before. Clean. Neat. A stage prop for a Franz Lehar operetta, even in the rain.

On a wooden sign, the word Buffet. Another sign: Waiting Room. A sign for Toilets and a sign for Ticket Office.

A hundred yards behind the picturesque station: a barbed-wire fence covered with pine branches.

Here too the hired Ukrainian mercenaries. The SS men, legs apart, their black uniforms shining in the rain. Off to the side, Ukrainians, clubs at the ready on their shoulders. A voice on the loudspeaker, casual, almost courteous, requests all new arrivals form two lines. Men to the right, women and children to the left.

As we are herded forward by the SS men and the guards, I receive several blows. But thanks to my experiences in the streets, I have learned how to protect my head. The blows fall on my upper arms and shoulders. Because I dodge, most of the blows glance off my body. Most.

I go to the right.

Other prisoners, earlier arrivals, already old hands, seem to be competing for prizes in a crazy race. They rush past us to pick up the luggage and parcels and whatever else has been carried to Treblinka by the Jews. I touch a man, for no other reason than to slow him down, to ask a question; but he throws off my hand, gives me a shove, and continues running.

The loudspeaker: *Get undressed. Have a shower. Then you'll be moved to your new work sites.*

As I go to an area where some men are already undressed, I see the train that has just brought us here starting to move out again. Men who have been cleaning it leap clear. The cars are empty. Returning to be filled again. Will the Jews be from Warsaw? Impossible. The Warsaw Jews have been exterminated. The new victims will be from other towns, other villages. By the time they arrive, I will be an old hand.

The loudspeaker: *Take your valuables and your papers. Don't forget your soap.*

SS men, whips in hand, move among the naked, tapping one or another, ordering them to put their clothes back on. They are taken away. I've not yet started undressing, and I don't intend to. Something stirs in my mind. Having heard stories about Treblinka, I know that only the naked are gassed. Remaining dressed offers better odds for remaining alive. At least remaining alive a bit longer. Time is important. Alive, I can take advantage of the slightest opportunity to escape.

As others remove their clothes, I act as if I'd been tapped by the whip. I nonchalantly join the line of men signaled out by the SS trooper. A risk. A gamble. But it pays off.

We are led away. An order is given. Immediately I am like that running man I'd tried to question, a runner myself. I follow the other runners, collecting luggage and parcels at the station, as well as the

132

site where the Jews who have marched to the showers have left their baggage behind.

We run.

Transferring luggage and bundles to the sorting lot where we open them. The contents, similar to the contents of millions of other parcels andsuitcases and bundles left in such sorting lots as Treblinka's, are dumped in their appropriate piles. Not piles but mountains.

Children's clothing. Little sweaters, a mountain of them. Coats, shirts, blouses: mountains of them. Shoes. Underwear. Bonnets. Crocheted booties. Leather lederhosen. Mountains, mountains.

Adults'. Divided into two areas, one for men, one for women. Every mountain built during that day or the last two or three days. Hats. Shoes. Socks. Underwear. Jackets. Spectacles. Pens. Flashlights. Dentures. Thirty, forty, fifty different items: thirty, forty, fifty different mountains.

The guards crack their whips. They control the snap so that it breaks at the correct moment, just at the surface of the skin. Specks of flesh are torn free.

A young man stumbles once, pauses to catch his

breath. One of the guards, reluctant to waste a bullet, kills him with blows of a rifle butt.

I run faster. Six SS men patrol the sorting areas with huge dogs, Dobermans. The dogs strain at their leashes, whining, pleading for the taste of a Jew. Occasionally, for no special reason, one of the dogs is unleashed to satisfy its appetite.

Three men, all older than I but probably in their early twenties, all of them pale, sickly looking, pause to support a fourth, who looks like a young Talmudic scholar. An SS man points his whip. Two guards step forward and shoot each of the four men twice.

I begin to stumble. How long have I been running? An hour? Five hours?

I cannot possibly stay erect any longer. I think of Rivka. How easily she slid beneath the sewage. I am sinking now. *Survive, Gideon.* I run. *Survive, Gideon.* I continue running.

The day ends. We line up, are given cans of water in which a few lumps of potato are floating. I pour some down my throat.

We run to our barracks.

So I am still alive.

In the fetid barracks I locate a wooden pallet on

which two men are lying. I stretch out, shoving to make space for myself.

There are six tiers of such pallets along the walls of the building, six pallets in each tier. Three pallets above ours, two below. It is dark. The man directly above me is shaken by an attack of dysentery. It leaks through the boards of his pallets. The stench is worse than the sewers. The potato water rises out of my stomach.

Darkness. Several men are praying. I try to turn on my side, but there is not enough room to manipulate my body. Sobs and groans overwhelm the sounds of praying. I pass in and out of spells of sleep. Each time I sleep, I am awakened by sounds I cannot identify but which, like huge strong hands gripping me, shake me and wake me up. In the morning, five bodies hang from the beams.

"Protect your face," a prisoner whispers as we begin running again.

Protect my face? What is so important about my face? Has he seen something there that requires protection?

More cattle cars have arrived. Sixty cars, each

of them packed with hundreds of Jews who are shoved, prodded, onto the platform.

Men to the right, women and children to the left.

I discover what that prisoner meant, that man who advised me to protect my face.

Guards carry whips of barbed wire. Those prisoners who cannot move fast enough, or who happen for any reason to aggrieve a guard, are flayed across the face. Now the *klepsydra,* the men who were flayed three or four days ago, have scarred faces that mark them for removal. They are shunted toward the loading area, are directed toward the building marked with the red cross. The *Lazarett.* The hospital.

Get undressed. Have a shower. Then you'll be moved to your new work sites.

I and others run to help those Jews who have just arrived. An old Hassid, his black clothes thick with grease, his prayer-shawl fringe showing beneath his coat, asks me in Yiddish what is happening. I scurry past him. Two young girls, with huge black eyes swimming in their round white faces, wait for my answer.

"It's all right," I say, astonished at the sound of my own voice. "It's all right. Don't be frightened."

I run again. Collecting. Sorting. Learning instantly how to run and at the same time probe pockets for concealed sugar cubes or bread crusts. Learning how to slip my treasures into my mouth without attracting the attention of the guards, who stroll everywhere with their long barbed-wire whips.

There is a road, an avenue, lined with tall dark pine trees. The *Himmelstrasse*. The Road to Heaven. I pick up papers, rags, whatever litter has been dropped by those who had been led along that road to another section of the camp.

I clean excrement and vomit from the walls and floors of the cattle cars so the next batch of victims will not be alerted to their fate before their arrival at the picturesque little train station. More and more Jews. Where do they come from? Will there never be an end to them?

I do not see them, I do not let myself see them, as Jews. If I see them as Jews, then I will have to see my own complicity in the crime. That would destroy me. I cannot be destroyed. Not by the Germans or the Ukrainians or by these Jews. I am meant to survive. To tell the story. To let the world know.

You must survive, Gideon. . . .

I run run run.

More *klepsydra* leave our unit, more victims for the *Lazarett*. No longer only those with scarred faces.

There are instantaneous, random choices now. A pause or a stumble: to the *Lazarett.* Slow down: to the *Lazarett.* Lift too small a load: to the *Lazarett.* Food in your mouth: to the *Lazarett.*

Sobs and groans and prayers every night. In the mornings, more bodies hanging from the beams.

I carry sacks of hair from the huts where the women had undressed and been shaven. The bald women had been led along the avenue of the dark pines, the *Himmelstrasse,* the Road to Heaven.

More piles growing into new mountains.
Jews now not just from Poland but from every part of Europe.
They carry their last possessions. Which are sorted. And piled.

I continue to escape the barbed-wire whips.
Survive, Gideon. Think only of survival. Do any-thing, *any*thing, to survive.

Cups, fragments of pottery, a silver fork, vases, cigarette cases, pocketknives, cigarettes, pipes, pencil stubs. And the photographs. Every photograph blending into every other. Every face blending into every other face. Every Jew like every other Jew. All Jews become one Jew.

The photographs are nothing but paper. No images of particular faces. Too dangerous. To stop and look, to try to identify—no, no time. I am nothing but a collection of bones and muscles that move. A machine. A machine without feelings, a machine in which no spring dare snap, no gear dare chip. I will function perfectly for years, if necessary, in order to survive.

Have I been here forever? Was there ever a ghetto? Did I ever have a mother and father? Who is Sonia? The name floats through my head without anchor to either face or body.

In a moment of reverie I pause, attracting the attention of a guard. The barbed wire lashes at my face. But I throw up a shoulder and succeed in deflecting the main force of the blow. I taste my own blood.

At night I mix the dirt of Treblinka's soil with spit, to make a paste that will conceal the cuts. No *Lazarett* for you, Gideon.

No *Himmelstrasse* for you, Gideon.

You cannot, will not, die here, Gideon.

139

13

In order to preserve my sanity, it is necessary not to see or understand what I do. Necessary not to *feel*. The more grotesque, the more dehumanizing the spectacle, the less I permit myself to see and hear. I become a robot.

I no longer consider myself a child. Nor am I considered a child by others.

The undressing job is assigned to me.

If one does not tyrannize his senses, does not control them, does not compel them to betray their natural normal performance, such jobs can be more exhausting than severe physical labor. But I refuse to see, to hear. I ignore questions, pleas, challenges.

Those who pause or delay, who ask questions, who ponder the strange events that have brought them here, these people have their clothing removed by force. By me.

When eyes peer into mine, seeking hope, my own eyes remain opaque, reflecting nothing back to the searcher. When an old, wrinkled hand tries to stop my fingers from loosening buttons, untying laces, I shake off the hand and rush the process along. Yiddish? Hebrew? Polish? German? English? No words in any language reach me. At night I talk to no one.

Any wonder that I, that any man, would turn away from such behavior? Try not just to deny it but to forget it?

It doesn't matter if the person is a man or a woman. When a woman pauses, tries to take time to soothe a troubled child, I rip her clothes from her body and run. I find the appropriate mountains. I run back to gather more clothing.

There are thousands of women. Numbers become insignificant. All ages, all shapes, from pale white to dark brown. They form, they are reduced to, one writhing mass. Not to one female but to one sexless mass. Who can notice, who can respond to a mass? A mass that stinks.

Days. I receive the kicks, the blows, the curses. Always protecting my face. I must weigh less than ninety pounds. But I insist on surviving. I would survive if I were ten pounds.

Darkness. The barracks.

In a far corner, a group of men gather to recite the evening prayer. I try not to sleep yet. If I fall asleep too early, I'll not be able to sleep later, as exhausted as I am. I stay awake so as to evade the dreams, the nightmares. Now many voices join in the Kaddish, the prayer for the dead. *Yiskadal veyis-kadash* . . .

I want to scream at the fools. Prayer will accomplish nothing; prayer will not save us. Guns. Only guns will save us.

I fall asleep. Refusing to pray for God's help. After all the prayers my mother and father sent to God, they were rewarded with betrayal. Why should I pray now to their God?

I am given a new job. Carrying stone, mixing concrete. A new building is being built between two barracks that house the Germans. All buildings at

Treblinka, except the gas chambers, are made of wood. There is much curiosity about the new building. The question is asked over and over, why should the Germans require concrete for this building when wood is so easy to obtain and cement so difficult?

A tall, soft-spoken man with dark hair, who reminds me of a distinguished university professor, asks me questions about the building. My name has been known since the day I arrived. This man, whose name is Galewski, has been kind to me. He knew my father. Not well, he said, when my father was alive, but better now since he was killed, the way he was killed. Galewski has been appointed *Lagerältester* by the Germans. He assigns work to us and sees to it that the work is performed properly. He is in charge of our *kapos,* our own policemen, and all of the foremen.

I do not know until I begin to write this book, until I read the various memoirs and historical accounts written by other survivors, that it is thanks to Galewski and a few others that there is an underground network at Treblinka. It is thanks almost exclusively to Galewski that the eventual revolt occurs. I remember him still, sitting with eight or ten other men, supposedly playing cards. The men talk in whispers about things other than the game. Often

143

cards are rejected or drawn or played without the slightest interest in their suit or value. The Ukrainians or Germans, when they appear, see nothing but a casual game of cards in progress.

Galewski, knowing I carry stones or mix concrete for the new building, asks me if I have seen any plans. How long is it? How wide? How tall? Are there to be windows? Where? Are there exits other than the main one? Have I heard the Germans or Ukrainians talking about the building? What do they say?

It is natural for Galewski to be curious, I am told. After all, he is an engineer.

For some time I have been collecting tobacco, a strand or a few flakes at a time, finding it among the lint in the seams of pockets. I have enough for five or six cigarettes. I do not smoke, but I know that some of the men would give their lives for a cigarette. I'll settle for a few potatoes, or a loaf of bread with, perhaps, a serving of butter and maybe even jam. Since I can now keep it down, I might even settle for six or seven rations of the potato soup.

As I saunter up to the card players, the conspirators, they break up. Casually, as if their distrust were of no significance to me, I announce that I have enough tobacco for five or six cigarettes. My mouth waters and my stomach growls in anticipation of a whole potato shared with no one. Maybe someone will have managed to steal an egg. After all, a few of the men have worked in the German officers' kitchen. Where there are officers, there are eggs; and where there are eggs, they can be stolen. Or bought. Yankele's voice comes back to me: "Everything, everyone has a price."

At my announcement, men crawl out of bunks, limp from the shadows, offering their prize personal possessions. There are promises of riches. Someone has gold hidden away, someone else diamonds. No one will admit he has hidden such a delicacy as an egg or a chunk of bread.

An enormous Hassid, a Biblical Jacob or Abraham, grips my arm and whirls me about so I can see a young man who is bent over his knees. The young man raises his head. I don't know him, but I see that he has been marked by the barbed wire. His nose has almost been ripped off. A deep gash stretches from chin to forehead. Tomorrow he will walk the *Himmelstrasse.*

I pull free of the Hassid's fingers. What do I care about the fate of this stranger? A man whose luck has run out. If it were my time, I'd not expect sympathy or request it. I open the negotiations, relying on cute little tricks I'd learned on the Warsaw streets. Talking singsong, showing the tobacco for only a moment, taunting, urging higher bids. But I have taken the Hassid's bait. I am trapped. I can't keep my eyes from the man sitting on his pallet. Finally, I slap the tobacco into the scarred man's hand.

A voice in my ear wakes me up. It is dark.

"You come from Warsaw."

"Yes." I try to slide back into sleep.

"You fought the Germans?"

"Yes."

"You know weapons? German weapons?"

"Yes."

"Are you willing to risk your life to escape?"

My heart leaps, races. Escape? How? We have no weapons. But the voice—is it Galewski's?—asked about weapons. We must have them. Not we but they. They, Galewski and his conspirators.

"Yes."

I hold my breath. Have I done the right thing? Galewski has been appointed by the Germans. He is in charge of all details. Is he a spy? A provocateur?

The man's hand gropes for my hand. We clutch each other's fingers.

I sleep, wake up to hear someone chanting Kaddish.

I will fight and escape and survive. My God, you have not forsaken me. I do not want to shout at the men who are praying.

14

From here on I write about the preparation for the rebellion at Treblinka. I took almost no part in the preparations, plans for which had been begun and reviewed and rehearsed long before I arrived.

After reading Jean Francois Steiner's *Treblinka,* and Alexander Donat's *The Death Camp Treblinka,* I realize what had preceded that terrible and beautiful day in August, 1943. Terrible because almost all the Jews who participated in the rebellion died; beautiful because a few, I among them, escaped.

Long before I arrived at Treblinka, a few men decided that vengeance upon the Germans, continued hatred and subsequent punishment of them, would not be enough. Killing Germans was only of immediate, momentary importance. What was needed was a variation of what had been needed at Warsaw, in the ghetto: a victory over the SS and a witness to tell the story, to describe the victory. The world—not just the Jews but the entire world—had to know that Jews were destroyed, that Jews not only fought back, but as they had for thousands of years, Jews survived. It was important that once again the word go out: the Jew has a covenant with God.

Who knows who first spoke of resistance? Who knows when the talk grew serious and a decision was made to prepare plans? It happened. One man, two men, a group of men. Possibilities were discussed, tactics designed.

At first, because the camp had such a mix of personalities, all of them with different impulses toward living and dying, and because spies were everywhere, Jew and non-Jew, a select few could be trusted. But as the debate and planning progressed, more and more prisoners had to be involved. A man who had been a professional soldier was designated military leader. Steiner refers to him as Djielo, others refer to him as Zelo. I do not recall the name but I do remember the figure. A man who talked and acted, and apparently thought, like a graduate of a military academy.

During the months in which I secluded myself here in my office, I not only wrote, I read. I guess I did not trust myself. Once I made that first move—to write my story for you and for myself—I was determined to tell the truth. At least what I perceived to be the truth. You can understand the difficulty by reading Donat's *The Death Camp Treblinka*. The six eyewitness accounts there are written by survivors. There is agreement on many details of the revolt, disagreement on a few. Some were involved in the planning of the revolt, some had no knowledge of it at all. When the shooting and burning began, escape was all that mattered. I had to escape, I was meant to survive.

The reading, of course, brought back many memories that I thought I had stored away in some vault in my mind. When that vault opened more than thirty years later, I found the memories fresh and alive. Too fresh, too alive.

To give you a sense not of my involvement but that of the soldier Djielo, or Zelo, of the careful planning that preceded the revolt, I quote now from

150

the last pages of chapter XIX of Jean Francois Steiner's *Treblinka*. I do not know how accurate a reconstruction it is but it serves to create a sense of the time and the place.

The problems of general strategy having been settled, Djielo proceeded to the immediate preparation of the revolt. He quickly outlined the method he had conceived for procuring weapons.

"Even if we manage to lure the SS to the tailor shops and kill them, we will not have many guns. Worse still, we will not have a single grenade. Now grenades would enable us to spread panic among the Germans and Ukrainians from the outset. However, there is a way to replace the psychological effect of grenades. It will require great coordination, but it is feasible. Adolf tells me that every week a special commando washes down all the barracks in the camp with a liquid disinfectant. This disinfectant is stored in the garage along with a number of barrels of gasoline. Rudek, the Jewish foreman of the garage, is one of the most reliable unit leaders. We did not want to ask for his consent before speaking to you, but Adolf assures me that he will agree. So either we would have to let the men in charge of the disinfection in on the revolt or"—Djielo turned to Galewski—"have our own men put in charge of this work."

Galewski nodded his head to indicate that it was workable.

"On D-day these men will fill their pails with kerosene instead of disinfectant and wash down all the barracks."

It was a brilliant presentation, and everyone could picture the camp being consumed by fire.

"The disinfecting takes place every Monday morning, so D-day will have to be a Monday.

"We have a few firearms at our disposal, so we will have to make a number of various sidearms like rods, shovels, and so forth: this will be the job of the iron and tin workers. In this connection Adolf has suggested the idea of making vitriol pistols out of rubber bulbs. There is plenty of vitriol in the camp, it will be easy. Well handled, it's an effective weapon. Those who possess them will have to stand beside a German or a Ukrainian a few moments before the launching of the attack and immediately spray him with vitriol and disarm him.

"Let us now proceed to H-hour proper.

"H-hour minus 60: The tailors and bootmakers kill their Germans and take their pistols, which they hide carefully.

"H-hour minus 5: The incendiary commando takes up positions near the barracks at a ratio of two men to a barracks.

"Each of the vitriol throwers picks out a German

or a Ukrainian. These men will have to be excellent shots, for their job will be to start neutralizing the watchtowers.

"A commando made up of particularly reliable men goes to the doors of the tailor and bootmaker shops and prepares to receive the weapons. Adolf will take personal charge of this commando.

"Finally, every man who is provided with a side arm or club unobtrusively picks out a German or a Ukrainian.

"H-hour: It would be unwise to choose a shot as signal to attack, because shots are heard every day in the camp. If we decide to take four o'clock as H-hour, the signal would be the whistle of the train that brings the prisoners back from the work camp. This detail will be worked out later.

"The first minutes will be the most crucial, for at that time we will be under fire from the watchtowers without being able to fire back. So, as the fire breaks out and the guards are attacked, Adolf's commando, armed with the weapons recovered from the Germans, will rush to the armory and take it by storm. Each man will grab a gun and take charge of one tower. Meanwhile the combat units will converge toward the armory to get weapons and will immediately take up their battle stations.

"The mass retreat will have to proceed to the south, in the direction of the forests. Two units, which will later act as scouts, will therefore head for the southern part of the camp while the other units will move to the west, the south and the east to protect the others.

"At this point the camp will be surrounded and reduced to cinders and to silence."

The evocative power of Djielo's voice was extraordinary. The other members of the committee looked at him, fascinated. This man seemed to them a messenger from heaven, a kind of angel armed with a flaming sword, come to lead them to victory. It was there, before their eyes, red as the burning of the camp, invincible as this archangel in battle dress.

"It is then that the third, and perhaps the most difficult part will begin: the withdrawal. At that moment we will be the masters of the camp, but the Germans will be starting to react. We can anticipate their counterattack in two phases. An immediate attack from the nearby garrisons will occur within the half hour. A second attack will mobilize much larger units and will probably take the form of a real combing of the region. If all goes well, we have nothing to fear from the first counterattack. Very likely the enemy reinforcements, not understanding very clearly what is going on, will converge on the camp in scattered formation. But since there are no garrisons between the forest and

154

the camp, the withdrawal will encounter no resistance from the front. Two combat units will be enough to guide the movement. The weight of the German attack will fall on the rear.

"We will join the battle in the camp itself to enable the mass of the prisoners to reach the forest. Then we will ourselves attempt a withdrawal movement. I will tell you frankly that this retreat in the open fields is against all instructions in the military manuals, and that the chances of success are extremely slim. We will undoubtedly beat off the first attack but what will happen afterward God alone knows.

"However, we may assume that the mass of the prisoners, guided by the two combat units, will meanwhile have reached the forests. Night will begin to fall, and it is doubtful that the heavy reinforcements who will then arrive on the scene will immediately launch a combing operation. As a rule you never comb at night, especially a forest. Besides, the Germans will not yet have recovered from their surprise, and they will have no accurate idea of the extent of our forces. We may therefore assume that, stunned by our resistance, they will prefer to use the night to prepare a vast search net and not start the combing operation until morning.

"Given the importance which the enemy will attach to recapturing all the prisoners, and allowing for the stupor he will feel, he will do everything in his power and will undoubtedly bring in tanks and armored cars. This probability means we will be in no position to fight the next day. So, once it reaches the forest, the troop will have to break up into many little groups, each of which will try to reach the heart of the forest separately. Some will be recaptured, but others will get away."

Djielo paused for a moment. Then he concluded in a curt and emotionless voice, "As for ourselves— well, I don't think our purpose is to save our own lives."

15

The armory, that building on which I've been working, has a massive door. Some survivors describe it
as metal. I recall it being of thick hardwood, rein-
forced by long belts of steel. Because of its size and
weight, it requires six of our biggest, strongest Jews
to carry it.

Every Jew who has been a carpenter or metal
worker is used by the Germans in constructing the
building. When the door is hung, under the watchful
eyes of Germans and Ukrainians, the sly locksmith
is able to steal ten seconds to slap a ball of soft
wax into the latch, to press it, to retrieve the wax.

Hours later, thanks to the craftsmen in the metal shop, Galewski possesses a key to the new arsenal.

We know the Germans are preparing to destroy Treblinka. The number of convoys and prisoners brought here each day has diminished. The camp was designed primarily to destroy the Jews of Warsaw. That design was efficient and successful. Other camps, larger and even more efficient, equipped with more advanced technology, have been constructed at sites more efficiently appropriate to the extermination of Jews of Romania, Latvia, Estonia, of Germany itself.

By gauging the size of the groups arriving now, the size of stockpiles of clothing and hair and teeth they produce, we estimate the camp will be destroyed in two or three weeks. Once the camp is gone, there will be no need to permit us to live on.

Soon after the armory is completed, a boy—a man of sixteen—who performs the role of valet for a German officer, uses the key. He inspects the armory, returns not just with the key but with the information that inside the building are automatic rifles, machine guns, an assortment of well-stocked weapon racks. And three wooden cases, each containing fifteen grenades.

We have a serious problem.

There are two camps in Treblinka. I, and the others in my barracks are in Camp 1. We know that Camp 2, at the other end of the *Himmelstrasse,* has approximately two hundred Jews who are literally being worked to death. Should we make contact with them, inform them of our plans? If we do not, they will be destroyed when our rebellion begins. If they cooperate and join the rebellion, our chances for victory will be improved. Is it worth the risk, informing those men, whom we do not know, who, because of their work, are nearly insane now, who might disclose the information about the rebellion?

It has been impossible to make contact with Camp 2. There are guards and wire barricades and guard dogs and the open *Himmelstrasse* between us.

Some argue that though we only have stories about what is going on in Camp 2, we do know that the workers are Jews; we are sure they are involved in the incineration of bodies. The stench forever in the air comes from Camp 2. The unmistakable stench of burning bodies. The Germans, we know, would not be doing the work with their own hands. Nor would the Ukrainians. They would be the camp guards.

159

Should we try to save those Jews at Camp 2, or let them be slaughtered? To try to save them would risk disclosure of our plans and the failure of the revolt. They would have to be informed of the plans and then have enough will to live so they might see rebellion as desirable. But each day of delay will improve the Germans' chances to discover our plans. Perhaps they already know. Perhaps one among us, intent on saving his own life, has already informed.

Finally there is general agreement. No choice. The Jews at Camp 2 must be involved. If they are not, their guards will be free to aid the guards here at Camp 1. We would be wiped out. As unfortunate men are transferred from Camp 1 to Camp 2 (one such unfortunate is Djielo), they agree to serve as missionaries for the cause.

The preceding details came to me from Steiner's and Donat's books. The details that follow came to me from one of the men who escaped from Camp 2 when the rebellion occurred.

The scent that is a nauseating presence at Camp 1 becomes thicker and sweeter with every step along the *Himmelstrasse* approaching Camp 2. Over and

160

above the scent is the sound of a motor. It never stops. It changes speed, it mumbles and roars and screeches, but it never stops. There is another sound that grows louder as Camp 2 is approached. The sound of fire. Of crackling flames.

The man who tells me about Camp 2 is to be my companion for a brief time after the rebellion. When the huge wooden gate at Camp 2, at the end of the *Himmelstrasse,* opens, my friend says that he actually cries out. It is a mix of anguish and disgust. His knees buckle. Everyone at Camp 1 has heard stories. But no one could have been prepared for this.

To the left, past the entrance, is a long ditch. Several excavating machines, the largest he's ever seen, lean out over the ditch, their long metal arms reaching out and down to tear at the yellow sand. At the end of each metal arm a metal fist, as large as an army tank, opens, thrusts itself into the sand, emerges as a closed fist. Inside the fingers are bodies dredged out of the sand. Fragments of bodies. As the great machines spin on their bases and the long metal arms swing around, human feet and hands and heads fall through the air. Extended over the bonfires, the metal fists open, dropping their contents into the flames.

Robots, robots with almost human faces, gather the fragments that have missed the flames and transport them as if they were logs or lumps of coal to the fires. The flames leap to grab the fragments.

A whip cracks. A rifle butt slams.

This is the land of the *Totenjuden.* The Death-Jews.

In the days that follow my friend sees several men break down, their robot circuitry cracking, sparking. For a moment they are human. Seeing, comprehending what they are doing, they go mad.

The men, my friend among them, work and run. They throw fragments of Jewish bodies into the flames. At night, while they struggle to sleep, the motors continue working, as do the flames.

Each day three or four men stop running, walk sleepily into the flames. Or, no longer running, but standing, staring, dumb, they accept a bullet at the back of the neck.

All the men surviving at Camp 2 have been beaten with whips and clubs and fists and boots since the day they arrived. But even here there are those who are less mad than others, men who, hearing the word *Jew,* seem to recall, if only for a moment, their

162

humanity. They brighten. They comprehend. Rebellion, yes. Vengeance, yes. Escape, yes.

On Friday, July 20, 1943, Camp 1 learns that the last ditch is being exhumed. The committee for the rebellion in Camp 1, knowing that the irrational men in Camp 2 cannot be restrained much longer, makes the decision. The day will be Monday, August 2. In thirteen days. It cannot be sooner. Too much has yet to be done. More weapons must be accumulated. It is discovered that the grenades in the armory don't have detonators. Participants will have to fashion their own weapons.

The ashes of the hundreds of thousands of corpses that have been burned are mixed with the soil. All traces of mass graves will be obliterated in a few days.

The soil is fertile. The entire area where once there had been nothing but corpses is leveled, seeded, and fenced with barbed wire. Pine trees are planted. And blue lupine. Like certain flowering plants, lupines constantly turn their leaves toward the sun.

16

Monday. August 2, 1943. I have been at Treblinka almost two months. Time no longer is divided into days and hours. It is only interruptions between long or short spans of despair.

Everyone, not just the trusted collaborators, senses that something important is about to happen, something that will convert despair into hope. Members of the committee are sober. In the stifling heat Germans as well as Jews seek refuge from the sun.

After much disagreement about the signal, it has been settled. A rifle shot. Risky, but too late to select and communicate a different one. The time: as close to four o'clock as possible.

The sun is blazing. Nothing moves. There is not even a breeze.

At three o'clock, following the plan that has been discussed and rehearsed—measured sometimes in minutes, sometimes in seconds—a few Jews force themselves to move. On the ground, near the watch-towers, gold coins glitter in their hands.

One by one, desire for gold blunting their fear of reprisals for a momentary relaxation of discipline, the sentries descend from their towers. There can be no danger. These Jews—weak, frightened, doomed—are too far gone to do more than buy a few hours extension of their miserable lives.

The small group of workers whose job is to disinfect bodies and buildings moves across the sun-drenched grass, carrying their buckets.

Even the usually alert German soldiers seem wilted, weakened by the sun.

The sentries approach the Jews, murmuring suggestions and promises and threats. The gold is flashed openly by the stupid and half-dead Jews, who obviously have gone crazy.

Because of the heat, everyone is permitted to rest during the worst part of the day. I lie on my wooden slat, silent like all the others. What is it? Something is about to happen and I don't know what it is. Does anyone else? The Germans? Now that the camp is nothing more than a flower garden, are the Germans about to kill us all?

Later I learn what has been happening while I lay there, waiting.

The assistant director of the camp appears, shouting. He charges into a barracks and comes back out, sending two prisoners sprawling in the dirt before him. They stand and empty their pockets.

The assistant director marches them toward the *Lazarett.*

A young Jew from Warsaw has one of the five rifles the committee has stolen from the armory just one hour before. He kneels at the corner of the barracks and aims his rifle.

The shot that echoes through the summer heat seems to me to have a quality about it unlike any shot I have heard in the ghetto or at Treblinka. The others seem to feel the same way. Everyone rushes outside, screaming.

The Camp 1 Jews, drawing concealed knives from their belts, using clubs, hammers, whatever they can grab, attack the sentries who have been mauling the Jews flashing the gold.

Every sentry is killed.

I run about, as do all the others, trying to make sense of the bedlam that has spread through the camp. A German runs around the corner of a barracks, firing a machine gun. He is swarmed over by Jews who are intent not so much on attacking him as on moving over him. He is in their way, between them and the forest that means freedom.

As Jews throw themselves at the inner ring of barbed wire, I see—one man, one action, separated from the chaos—someone, it could be Galewski, running toward an armored car that is always positioned near the building that houses German guards.

The man survives the first burst of fire that comes from the Germans in the building, but then he stumbles. He falls, rises, runs on. Jews who have picked up rifles fire at the windows of the building. I pick up the German machine gun—its owner has been trampled to death—and shoot through window after window.

The Jew is up the side of the car and over the

edge and inside the turret. I continue firing. The turret slowly rotates. The barrel of the car's heavy machine gun is pointed now not at the Jews but at the German barracks.

Just as the action of the man who captured the armored car had been distinct, so there is now a sound remembered forever. The Germans cry out before they die.

My machine gun is either jammed or not functioning. I throw it away and join the others who are fleeing the camp. The bedlam is now outlined in flames. Every building on the grounds seems to be on fire.

As I move across the barbed wire, I have to use the bodies of Jews who are sprawled there, dead, as mats. Ahead of me, bodies are hanging from another wall of wire. Bodies of Jews who made it this close to freedom before they died.

Beyond the wire, people are running across the field.

Everything described has occurred not in minutes, but in seconds. The Ukrainians and the Germans, as well trained as any humans can be, are now starting to respond. But the shock has been so great that the response has been delayed seconds too many.

One by one several watchtowers and the barracks catch fire, burn, collapse in an eruption of red cinders and black smoke.

I run. Desperation gives me energy. I glance back. The camp is in flames. Bodies cover the grounds, the barbed wire, the fields. As I enter the forest, I glance back one more. The sky is black with smoke. The red flag with the black swastika sails above the water tower.

Gasping, my legs melting beneath me, I drop to the ground.

Around me are the survivors, inert, unconscious, trying to regain enough strength to move deeper into the forest.

I open my eyes and see the water tower spurt flame. The red flag with the black swastika dips, catches fire, disappears.

Almost all of the committee that planned the rebellion die there, at Treblinka. Approximately six hundred of the fourteen hundred prisoners who were at the camp at the beginning of the rebellion escape into the forest.

Of those six hundred, many of whom join the Polish underground army, there are forty survivors when the war ends in 1945.

Of the forty who survive the end of the war, the great majority now live in Israel. Others are scattered across the world.

I team up with a survivor about my age. It is he who tells me about those last weeks at Camp 2. He had been there, burning bodies. Like me, he knew little of the plans for rebellion. Like me and many others, when the time—the day, the hour, the minute—arrived, we ran as if we knew what was happening.

Later my friend and I join the Polish underground army, other Jews tell me that Djielo, or Zelo had been killed in an uprising. He sacrificed himself, one of them said. He did not expect to survive.

The first week the two of us, asleep in a hut, hear three Polish soldiers outside the door in a drunken babble. They are making plans to knife us to death. My friend has a wristwatch he has managed to conceal all through the ghetto and the work camps and Treblinka. They mean to take it.

He and I leap through a window. He breaks his leg. I do not realize he is not running behind me as I crash through the brush. When I discover I am alone, I run back. The Poles are gone. My friend, who had survived the labor camps and the death camps and the rebellion at Treblinka, is dead. His hand, as well as his watch, is gone.

17

I cross the Bug River.

The fields are covered with stubble now and the wind is harsh. At night the puddles in the muddy roads are covered with a thin scum of ice.

I sleep during the day, walk at night. A few times, there are German patrols on the roads, but I avoid them. Only once does a soldier fire at me. Lying in a ditch, I hear men laugh at their comrade who has fired at trees three nights in a row now.

Occasionally I put in a day or two of work on a farm. Washing down horse or cow stalls, shoveling grain, hauling wood.

After months of aimless wandering and day-today jobs, I find myself near the village of Nowy. Grandmother was born here. I yearn to stay. Perhaps she has survived and will return eventually. Will she bring Sonia with her? I hover at the edge of the village for days, hiding, as if by being near my grandmother's birthplace I will just naturally be safer, happier.

I approach a family. I have eaten nothing for two days. I have not slept even during the day, because of the cold.

Yes, there is work I can do. Most of the young men have gone or been taken by the Germans. People make way for me, wonder about me, consider me with open distrust. I can see them wondering why I have survived, why I am not fighting or dead.

The first night, sitting at the table with the family, I try to swallow the potatoes and the thick chunks of bacon. I gag on the bacon. I eat nothing but bread and potatoes and a mug of cold milk.

I leave late on the second night. I cross the Bug River again, fording the icy stream in the darkness, clinging to logs in the deepest parts. When I reach the outskirts of Warsaw, I know that since my escape from Treblinka, this is where my heart has been guiding my body.

Night. The Warsaw streets are quiet, empty. The

long war has taken its toll. Now the Gentiles are hiding from the Germans, hoping to escape the labor camps. Word has gotten out—I heard the news in the forests, from Polish partisans—that now not just Jews are perishing in the death camps. Gypsies, Catholics, Communists, Socialists, labor leaders, intellectuals. And, as the Germans call them, those stupid Slavs. Others than Jews are now walking down their own *Himmelstrasse*.

In the streets, old secrets reveal themselves. All my senses are mobilized. I remember alleys, doorways I'd long forgotten. I know how to merge with shadows. But a voice, the sound of what might be a boot, the throb of a motor throws my body into trembling, sends me into hiding.

Daylight approaches. I watch them pass, those supermen, wondering what they had talked about that night in early August when hundreds of their fellow supermen had been outwitted and outfought by a ragtag army of emaciated, half-dead Jew bandits.

For a moment, as I see and hear them pass by, their rasping guttural voices chopping at the air, the urge returns. If I only had a rifle . . . But enough! I am in search of life, not death.

The stairway twists along its old familiar spirals. As I climb, alert for the slightest noise above or below me, I hold back my tears. I can feel the body of my little sister in my arms; I can smell the lilac scent of Grandmother.

The soft tap on Grandmother's door silences the voices on the other side. I tap again.

Silence.

"It's me, Grandma. Gideon."

The door opens, a crack. I push it farther, my arms out to catch Sonia. My arms fall. The person at the door and the people behind him are strangers. But there, against the wall, is Grandmother's velvet sofa. Beside it Grandmother's pale blue wing chair from America. I, and my father, have sat in that chair a thousand times. I, and then Sonia, have slept on that soft sofa.

An old woman? A child? No, there's no old woman here. And no child.

Have they moved? Does anyone know . . . ?

Wait, an old man says. Yes, an old woman had lived here. Before. A child, too. A little girl. Some time ago.

The old man, a gray-haired worker with swollen

hands, hops about on one foot, the right one. The left leg is off at the knee.

Tell me more. Where are they?

Oh, they're long gone. The Germans . . . the *Umschlagplatz* . . . an informer. Terrible days, these are terrible days. Yes, he remembered the old woman. Not a bad person, for a Jew. Terrible days.

I knock on the door. It cracks, opens wide.

One-Eye looks well fed, almost cherubic. He studies me and then, with a wide grin that shows three front teeth missing, he grabs me in a bear hug. I fall into his arms. We are both weeping. We hold on to each other.

I stay with One-Eye, hiding day and night in his apartment. Never going outside, not even at night.

Weeks. Months. A year and a half.

One-Eye comes and goes. He supplies food, clothes, books. He never asks questions, never criticizes, never urges me to go for a walk in the sweet spring air.

The others in the gang? All are dead.

Two weeks after the war ends, One-Eye introduces me to a friend. A woman comes with a camera.

176

She takes my photograph. I write my name on a piece of paper that she takes with her. On the paper I have recorded necessary information. False, of course. Three days later the identification and employment cards arrive. They have been "aged" to look heavily used.

One-Eye, saying he has never been richer, pays. I go out into the streets. We work together, peddling false papers. I earn enough to go to a doctor. Asking no questions, he removes the tattooed number from my arm.

Our last night together, we go out to dinner.

I can now eat rich food and keep it down. Afterward, in the street, we embrace again and bid each other good-bye.

Alone, in the light cast by a bonfire kept alive by children, I examine my forged papers again. I am Jon Pedderson. Your father.

The sergeant in the office is from—where else?—Brooklyn.

He is a Jew. He speaks Polish. I do too, affecting what I believe to be an appropriate accent.

Where, he asks as he prepares to type, where was I born?

I close my eyes and begin the lie that is to live for thirty-three years. "Denmark."

The Polish Jew from Brooklyn glances up from his typewriter. His mouth is open, as if he is about to deny my plot. Then his mouth closes and his shoulders drop and he starts typing. "Birthplace," he murmurs, as his fingers tap the keys, "Denmark."

Give me your tired, your poor, the Statue of Liberty says. *Your huddled masses yearning to breathe free, The wretched refuse of your teeming shore, Send these, the homeless, tempest-tossed, to me: I lift my lamp . . .*

Oh, Mother. Oh, Father. Sonia, Grandmother. Oh . . .

I lift my lamp.

Oh, Jews . . .

. . . beside the golden door.

18

Orinda, California
July 20, 1978

It is finished.

I wanted to stop many times during these months I've been writing. Perhaps I would again stop remembering, I told myself, if I stopped writing. But only God can calm a flood by pointing at the tumbling water and commanding it to stop.

I have succeeded so long in not remembering that often I wonder if what had just appeared on the

179

page was fact or fiction. I needed only to look at my arm. There is the evidence. Fact.

That Holocaust series on television did not tell my story.

I knew then it had to be told. You might wonder why I didn't confide all of this then. I could not. I did not know until after I started writing, what "all of this" meant, what "all of this" would include.

I began by reading books written by Jews who had survived. Martin Gray and Max Gallo's *For Those I Loved.* Alexander Donat's *The Holocaust Kingdom* and *The Death Camp Treblinka. The Stars Bear Witness* by Bernard Goldstein. *The Bravest Battle* by Dan Kurzman.

Those and others. Why did I read? Because I could not rely on memory. I had betrayed my memory. Why shouldn't it betray me?

As I read, the barriers in my memory began to tumble. I had witnessed you, Maggie, and you, my children, relying on others to tell you my story. I had to tell it. If I didn't, I was robbing all of you of your husband's, your father's, your own, past.

As I neared the completion of this writing I considered having that number tattooed on my forearm again. But this time I would be paying some unconcerned American to apply a number on my skin.

The number's gone but the arm's still there. Oh, the joy with which it reaches out now to embrace you all.

Your husband, your father,
Gideon Malinovsky